DAWN ARRIVES

DAWN ARRIVES

THE SECOND DARK AGES™ BOOK FOUR

MICHAEL ANDERLE

ELL LEIGH CLARKE

Beta Editor / Readers
Bree Buras (Aussie Awesomeness)
Tom Dickerson (The man)
S Forbes (oh yeah!)
Dorene Johnson (US Navy (Ret) & DD)
Dorothy Lloyd (Teach you to ask...Teacher!)
Diane Velasquez (Chinchilla lady & DD)

JIT Beta Readers

James Caplan
Joshua Ahles
Sarah Weir
Kimberly Boyer
Paul Westman
Peter Manis
Thomas Ogden
Larry Omans
Kelly O'Donnell
John Ashmore
Sherry Foster
Veronica Torres
Timothy Bischoff
Edward Rosenfeld
Micky Cocker

If I missed anyone, please let me know!

Editors
Stephen Russell
Lynn Stiegler

CHAPTER ONE

<u>**Yokohama, Japan, Yokohamakeon (Park)**</u>

The park was peaceful.

Serene, even.

Sunlight kissed the lawn and littered the trees, casting intricate patterns beneath the leaves.

The black box touched down lightly in the square. It had been several days since it had been here…not that anyone had noticed.

Sabine was the first to step outside and gaze at the wonder of the world. The whirlwind tour of Europe had been mind-blowing, or at least it would have been for her old self. Her new self took it in stride, as simple as breathing or shooting a gun…which were on a par for her at this point.

She wandered around the area, examining it through her nanocyte-enhanced eyes. Her wounds had completely healed, leaving her beyond grateful for her new lease on life. She looked several decades younger, and was more powerful than she had ever been.

She sensed Akio landing in the fighter Pod next to the box, and she smiled. He got out of the ship, as calm and stoic as ever.

They exchanged a glance. An acknowledgment.

Sabine glanced at the sky, inhaling the atmosphere and appreciating every bit of what her senses were taking in.

Michael ambled out just then, removing his hat to scratch his head and then replacing it.

Yuko, Eve, Jacqueline, and Mark followed in close succession.

Jacqueline was the first to suggest the specifics of their first mission, since her were-body craved food. "So, what about the breakfast place just across the park we found last time?"

Michael looked at Akio. *As long as there is meat. I could murder a steak right now.*

Hai.

"Out loud, boys!" Sabine reminded them, tilting her head at the others.

Akio shot across to Michael, *she can read our thoughts?*

Michael shrugged. "Do they have steak?" he asked Jacqueline.

She grinned. "You bet your hat they do...and since when do you eat?"

Michael started walking toward the restaurant. "I could do with something. Haven't eaten since I nearly got torn apart in the Etheric, and I have a hankering for something with iron in it."

Mark slung his arm around Jacqueline's shoulder and followed. Eve closed up the box and joined the group as they made their way across the lawn, happy and peaceful for the first time in a long while.

Sabine quietly followed, looking at everything as if she were seeing with new eyes.

Steaks and mountains of other breakfast foods later, Michael pushed his plate aside and regarded Yuko quietly. Yuko noticed his regard and stopped eating.

"I suppose we should talk about what's next," Michael ventured.

Yuko nodded. "I'm guessing getting back to BA is still the priority?"

Michael dabbed his mouth with his napkin. "It is."

Yuko looked at the ceiling, arranging her thoughts. "Well, we know the locations of the boxes. Five are in our secret storage." He glanced at Akio, who nodded. "And the other eleven will be wherever the map says they are."

Michael considered the options. "We will need engineers and scientists to put it together," he mused, and gestured to Akio. "We've been talking about it. Locals with the technical skills we need would be our best bet, but they lack honor. Many will try to steal what they can if we keep them in Japan."

Yuko filled in the blanks. "So you're thinking you want to recruit them here and take them to an isolated location to work?"

Michael bowed his head and glanced around, reading the other customers' minds to make sure their conversation wasn't being monitored.

Jacqueline finished her last bite and swallowed, then leaned against Mark and stared down at his plate. When he looked at her, she smiled at him. "So, are you stuffed? Are you done with that bacon, then?"

Mark pushed his plate over to his girlfriend with a smile. "Knock yourself out."

Jacqueline rested her knee against his under the table.

Michael pulled out the tablet he'd been using in the Pod, and after flicking it on he pointed to the screen. "Where are the burial sites on this map?"

Eve quietly responded, "China. If you want to stay there, I will find a suitable location for your scientists to work."

Michael nodded and got up, his brows still drawn together in thought. "Very good. Let's make that happen." He turned to Eve. "Please put the word out that we need the best tech engineers, inventors, and scientists to put together an experimental machine."

Eve grinned. "Got it. We'll have something set up within the day."

Yuko hesitated. "So, uh, who will run the interviews?"

Michael looked at Eve and Yuko. "Go, team?" he suggested hopefully as a small smile grew on the sides of his lips.

Yuko shook her head firmly. "We need to be sensible about this. If we want to shorten the critical path, might I suggest you and Akio handle the recruiting? Mind scans and all that *could* be helpful."

Akio's face remained expressionless. "But technology is *your* thing."

Excellent response, Michael sent to Akio, his eyes giving nothing away as he continued to look at Yuko.

I am trying, Akio replied. His face gave nothing away to Sabine.

Eve chimed in, "I can run thorough enough background checks from here before we even see them to find out if they are capable. We only need to meet them so they can get to know us and find out who they'll be working for. Well, and for you two to do your mind-reading thing." She looked from Akio to Michael.

Akio shrugged, allowing a half-smile to grace his lips as he glanced at Michael. "Guess we've got our next mission."

Michael sighed, stepping away from the table and shoving the chair back under it. "Well, if any of them piss me off I reserve the right to—"

Jacqueline raised an eyebrow and Michael stopped talking as he regarded the young woman, who had finished Mark's plate as well. "Go ahead," she said. "I'm listening. Oh...and did I mention I'm sooooo looking forward to meeting Bethany Anne?"

Michael crumpled. "Well, fine." He looked around, resigned. "Maybe I'll spend the rest of the day blowing off some steam, then."

Jacqueline chuckled. "Looks like he's all antsy after that last operation."

Mark started chuckling, but was quickly silenced by a glare from the Dark Messiah.

"So unfair how you girls get away with—" No one heard the rest of the sentence, since Michael had disappeared.

Akio placed his eating utensils on the table and got up.

"I'll make sure he stays out of trouble," he said as he stepped away from his chair.

Eve called after him, "If you need a battle range we can arrange for something in the Tech Palace. You know, some realistic simulations of ancient battles from Earth's history."

Akio looked impressed, and he bowed slightly. "Let me talk to him." And then he vanished out the door, the ringing bell as the only hint he had been there.

The team looked at the empty space where Michael had been.

Mark nudged Jacqueline. "Did he just..." he whispered, his eyebrow raised.

Jacqueline nodded.

Mark set his teacup down. "And all that about not drawing attention to—"

Jacqueline patted his leg under the table. "It's a do-as-I-say-not-as-I-do kinda thing, honey." She paused ever so slightly. "You'll get used to it."

Sabine sipped her tea, contemplating something that made her eyes defocus and look dreamy.

"You ok?" Jacqueline asked her.

"Huh, what? Me? Yeah, fine..." she muttered, only half-aware that the others were looking at her.

<u>Tokyo, Japan</u>

"It's all set up," Eve told Michael. The Pod had landed in a small, protected lot. "All you have to do is show up at this address at ten o'clock and..." she waved her fingers in the direction of Michael's head, "do your thing."

Michael took the piece of paper she handed him as he eyed her. "And you're sure these front-office people helping us during the recruitment know what they're doing?"

"Absolutely." She nodded. "And if you have any doubts, Akio can ping me and we will sort it out remotely."

Michael didn't look convinced. In the last recruitment drive he had been part of, Bethany Anne and her team had gotten everything done. "Man, that woman knew how to get shit done…" he mumbled.

Eve heard every syllable, but chose not to pry. Even though they had a special connection now, she didn't really want to start probing her new "father" about her…well, would she be called "Mom?" Or maybe "Stepmom?" She shook her head, confused by the organic designations. If she ever saw ADAM again—or rather *when,* she corrected herself—she would be sure to ask him.

The box was a hub of activity. They had spent the whole of yesterday back in normality, and it was now time to leave for another adventure.

Or rather, head for an excavation—in China.

"I didn't know China existed before the other day," Mark was saying as he passed Jacqueline a stack of blankets to stow.

"Right, and all courtesy of the School of Michael." She grinned and said, "Right, Sabine?"

"Huh?" Sabine looked up from the computer she was sitting behind.

"We get to travel and see the world, thanks to Michael."

"Yeah. Yeah, it's amazing." Sabine smiled absently,

clearly a million miles away. She shook her head and came back to the present. "Do you need me to do anything?"

"Nope, we're all good. We'll be ready to go as soon as Yuko gives the word."

Sabine glanced at Akio, who was standing by the doorway, with sadness in her eyes.

Jacqueline noticed, but said nothing.

Within twenty minutes, everything had been squared away and the plans laid out. The box lifted from the park and disappeared.

Akio mouthed, "Be safe, young one," then became aware of Michael heading toward him across the lawn.

He glanced at a spot of blood on Michael's shirt. "I thought those simulations were…simulations? As in, there was nothing to kill?"

Michael grinned as he approached Akio. "Nothing to worry about. Just, some punk tried to start something, so I provided him with an opportunity to never do it again."

Akio looked down at the shirt, and then back up as the two started walking down the sidewalk. "You killed him?"

Michael shook his head. "No, not at all. I just smacked him in the mouth and walked away. No Mysting. It was…*helpful.*"

Akio shook his head, closing his eyes in dismay. "The sooner we get you off-world and back to Bethany Anne, the better…sir."

Michael chuckled dryly as he looked at the architecture around them, much of which was new to him. "Agreed. Now, how about we go recruit some tech-heads to help us with that?"

They headed back across the street, enjoying the pleasantness of the city before they had to mind-read a bunch of imbeciles. Yuko had given them very strict instructions not to kill anyone.

This was going to be a challenge.

In Transit between Tokyo and an Undisclosed Location in China

Mark watched carefully over Yuko's shoulder as she and Eve ran the analysis on the data he'd pulled in the bunker.

"So we have sixteen of these things to dig up?" He ruffled his hair as if ready to tear it out. "Do we know how deeply they're buried?"

Eve raised a finger. "Probably around ten feet, but maybe more."

Mark pushed out his bottom lip, not happy at the prospect of the sheer amount of digging that lay ahead of them.

"And," Eve continued, "it's not sixteen."

Jacqueline was lounging on a bunch of blankets at the other end of the cabin. "I'm sure Yuko said sixteen when she was explaining this to me...with the Kurth-ery-what-nots."

Yuko didn't take her eyes from her analysis, but Eve poked her head around the monitor to look at the Were girl. "That is the total, but we intercepted five before they were buried and have them in a secure location."

Jacqueline looked impressed.

'That's something," Mark agreed. "Please tell me you have equipment, though. For digging?"

Yuko shook her head and patted Mark's six-pack. "That is why we brought our strongest vamps and Weres." She chuckled quietly, glancing briefly at Sabine. Their newest recruit was sitting quietly at the far end of the room stroking a knife against her index finger.

Sabine didn't react, and the conversation moved on.

Mark's eyes flicked back to the screen to try to make sense of the map. "So how do we figure out which ones were intercepted?"

Yuko shrugged. "I'm trying to remember."

Eve smiled quietly at the other console. "I'm running an analysis based on where the interceptions took place. It'll be done in a few minutes."

Jacqueline glanced around the cabin. "So how big are these crates? Are they going to fit in here?"

Yuko rolled her lips together. "Probably not. We can tow them with the box's winch, but we should probably move them at night." She jerked her thumb in Eve's direction. "Eve will be able to coordinate with the local satellites so we're not picked up on camera or radar."

Eve clarified, "And by 'coordinate' she means I'll block them from seeing us or sending any data which gives us away."

Jacqueline nodded her head, thinking about the enormity of what they were about to do. "And transport these boxes...where?"

Eve took that question. "I'm analyzing sites right now. We're looking for somewhere that has amenities nearby for the workers—housing, food, and so on—but is out of the way of prying eyes." She paused as her eyes flicked unnaturally for a moment. "I estimate that to optimize our travel with the crates and reduce the probability of being seen, we're probably looking at somewhere on the outskirts of China itself."

Mark stepped away from the consoles and ambled over to where Jacqueline was sitting on the floor. "I understood that China was like, I dunno…the ass-end of nowhere?"

Yuko nodded. "I know. You get all the rough missions."

Mark continued to gripe. "While Michael and Akio get to sit around in Luxury World playing mind-games and VR!"

Yuko nodded in agreement and turned to Eve. "I think he was looking forward to getting back to the Tech Palace."

Eve's voice was filled with pride when she said, "I think so too." She called to Mark, "Is it the simulations or the cotton candy you miss most?"

Mark sighed before he chuckled. "All of the above!"

Jacqueline leaned into him and he put his arm around her shoulders. "I hope we get to visit it one more time before we leave Earth," she mumbled into his t-shirt.

Mark glowed. That meant they were going with them. Off-world. In that moment, he swelled with happiness.

Life really cannot get much better than this, he thought to himself as he gave his girl a squeeze.

CHAPTER TWO

<u>Shimpo-Ra Memorial Hall, Tokyo, Japan</u>

Akio glided quietly back into the room, footsteps whispering over the lacquered floor, and sat behind the desk next to Michael. They were presently waiting for the next candidate in the sports hall Eve had booked for the recruitment drive.

We should have organized an assistant too, he shot to Michael. *Walking back and forth to fetch people is tedious.*

The ArchAngel smirked. *Ah, it's beyond you now, is it my friend? Now that you've faced down the demons of the planet you're above such things?*

Akio' eyes danced with humor. *Not in the slightest. But what is the point in spending a hundred and fifty years honing one's ability to mind-read and enter buildings like the wind and still be required to perform the mundane tasks?*

Michael smirked at Akio as the new candidate, who had just completed his journey across the twenty-yard space between them and the door, sat nervously in the chair across from them.

Akio rearranged his robe as he crossed one leg over the other and both men pursed their lips, saying nothing.

The candidate shifted uncomfortably in the prolonged silence.

"Aren't you going to ask me any questions?" he asked, pushing his tech-enhanced glasses back onto his nose and fidgeting. His mouth was dry. It didn't take a Dark Messiah to know he was nervous.

Michael, now deadpan, looked down at his fingers, inspecting the cuticles. *I dunno what to ask him. You ask him something.*

Akio stifled a chuckle but remained composed—not that the candidate would have noticed. "I read on your resume that you have an interest in experimental technology. Would you like to expand on that a little?"

The candidate, having finally been acknowledged by the strange duo who were supposed to be interviewing him, launched into a discourse on how he'd been involved in helping stabilize the coherence of the qubits in quantum computing and how great strides had been made during his tenure as a volunteer at some center or another.

Michael's eyes glazed over. *He's clean. We knew he was clean. Why did you have to get him started? Do you secretly hate me? Have I done something to you lately I need to apologize for?*

Akio maintained his feigned interest in the candidate. *You told me to ask him a question.*

Michael audibly sighed. *Yeah, something like, "What year did you graduate from school?" Not something he's obviously not going to stop talking about.*

Akio's mental voice came back laced with humor. *Well, how about next time* you *ask the question?*

Ten long minutes later the candidate stopped talking, messed around with his glasses, and looked nervously from one interviewer to the other. He finally rested his eyes on the Stetson on the table.

"Is that—" He stopped himself.

He's found a spot of blood on my hat.

Akio chuckled mentally at the scientist sitting across from them in the cold, unimpressive hall. *Make him an offer. It will distract him.*

Michael leaned forward, which pulled the candidate's gaze from his bespoke Stetson. "We're impressed with you, and we'd like to offer you a job. We'll give you a ten percent increase over your existing salary. Job starts tomorrow." He paused a moment, then verified, "You're ok with traveling to another location for the assignment?"

The candidate swallowed hard, scrambling to take it all in. "Er, yes, sir."

Michael smiled. "Good, then. Report back here at ten tomorrow morning. And send the next person in, please. Save this old man from having to get up and walk across the hall," he added, indicating Akio.

Akio narrowed his eyes at Michael, which caused the candidate to relax a little.

Maybe they are human after all, he thought.

Then he noticed that the two men's eyes were dancing with amusement.

Can they read my thoughts? he wondered, freaking out as he scrambled back across the expanse of the hall to the safety of the corridor beyond.

The door clunked closed behind him, leaving the two vampires in silence.

Michael broke the silence. "This is turning out to be much more fun that I thought it would be."

"*Hai*," Akio agreed. "Much better."

Undisclosed location, Tokyo, Japan

Raiden whistled as he sat at his multi-screen computer array.

Kuro strode into the office, his laptop slung over his shoulder. He was carrying a flask of something hot.

Before he even took his jacket off he turned to Raiden, who wasn't even wearing his headphones. "What's gotten into you?"

"What do you mean?" Raiden asked.

Kuro eyed him, "You're decidedly...chirpy."

"Well, my friend," Raiden confessed, swiveling around to brag, "you're looking at the genius who has figured out that not only is there a connection between the ArchAngel our sources had been tracking and the Diplomat, but—"

Raiden turned to the array of monitors when a screen beeped, then back to Kuro once again.

Kuro's face was expressionless. He would reserve his judgment while he heard the update.

"I have also found an 'in,'" Raiden finished.

There was a slight tick in the corner of Kuro's right eye when he replied a moment later, "An *in*?"

"*Hai*." Raiden nodded. "Exactly. It looks like the Diplomat is recruiting specialists in experimental tech. Sound interesting?"

Kuro's eyes narrowed. "She's looking for people who can help her put it all together, which means—"

Raiden waved his hand. "Which means she probably also has the map...and that's ok. We can insert our scientists and engineers into the operation to keep an eye on things as they develop...and swoop in when the time comes."

Kuro leaned his backside against the window ledge, quietly putting his laptop on the ground by his feet. He didn't have a desk in this empty apartment they were using. "But what about the locations? Your plan is only good if we don't intercept the packages first."

Raiden sat back in his seat, grinning confidently. "I also have that one handled. This is my sneaky backup plan, since Plan A is already in play."

Kuro was reluctant to let Raiden take the lead on this, but he kept it to himself. It might be useful to let him handle things and limit his own exposure...as long as it wasn't at the expense of the ultimate goal.

"Tell me about your Plan A, then," Kuro urged his partner.

"Well, we have the locations and we can pretty much guess that they're going to show up at the sixteen spots, so I had your guy Benjiro station one man at each location. When we have a sighting, Benjiro will swoop in and take them out."

Kuro slowly spoke once Raiden was done. "In which case your resident spies are useless."

Raiden nodded, still smiling confidently. "Agreed, but this wouldn't be the first time the Diplomat has taken out a whole team of assets."

Kuro bobbed his head, his eyes drifting to a spot on the floor in front of him. "So your plan is to...what, just take them out, then have the remaining team members go dig up the other fifteen locations?"

Raiden nodded. "*Exactly.*"

Kuro's face showed visible expression now…perhaps deliberately.

"And Benjiro knows your plan?" he asked.

"Of course," Raiden answered. "He had to know everything to make the best decisions, right?"

Kuro sighed, more to himself than anything. "If you were Benjiro, when do you think you'd take the Diplomat out?"

Raiden thought about this a moment before shaking his head. "I'm not following."

Kuro spoke slowly. "Well, if you knew that you had to take the Diplomat and her team out and once you had accomplished this your team would have to do all the work to acquire the treasures, when would it be best to take them out?"

The question confused Raiden.

Kuro shook his head. "What I'm trying to get at is that if I were Benjiro, I would wait until the Diplomat has retrieved all the boxes and *then* take her out."

Raiden's eyes widened. "At which point, if Benjiro fails we have little opportunity to correct the problem—and she potentially gets away with all the pieces."

Kuro pursed his lips, still nodding.

Raiden smacked his palm against his head. "Dammit," he spat, scrambling for his keyboard. "I'll have him make a move as soon as possible. Tell him we have a deadline in the next twenty hours."

Kuro picked up his laptop case and wandered over to

the sofa where Orochi normally sat. "Sounds like a plan," he agreed, mulling the impact of Raiden's actions on his personal plans.

"Incidentally," Kuro called across the room, "who are you using for the China op?"

Raiden stopped what he was doing again and turned around again. "Feng's old team," he said brightly. "Figured they were qualified and motivated, and since Orochi took him out there were whole squadrons without a mission, just waiting to be bought off."

Kuro maintained his composure. "With my money?"

Raiden looked flustered. "*Our* money," he corrected. "The money we agreed to collectively allocate to this...investment."

Kuro nodded. "Yes, of course."

"Thought you liked it when people showed initiative," Raiden muttered as he turned back to his screens.

Kuro didn't answer, just sat down on the couch and opened his laptop.

CHAPTER THREE

<u>Site One, China</u>

Mark straightened and wiped his brow. The sun was high in the sky. They had started at first light, and it was now too hot to be doing such physical work.

"My idea of physical labor is replacing the hard drive in an old computer," he muttered.

He dropped his shovel and pulled his t-shirt over his head. It was already damp with sweat, but at least it wouldn't be clinging to him.

He felt eyes on his naked back, and when he turned Jacqueline was enjoying his vampire musculature. He grinned at her, and she smiled back and continued to dig.

Sabine was working next to her. They'd been bonding over girl talk, speaking of things which Mark had no reference points from which to add to the conversation.

Sabine sighed as she looked at the pile of dirt she and Jacqueline had cleared, then scanned the landscape while allowing the faint breeze to cool her.

"You ok?" Jacqueline asked.

"Yeah," Sabine said. "Just promised myself that I'd take more time to appreciate this place."

"On account of you nearly dying?" Jacqueline ventured.

Sabine nodded. "That too. But also... Well, if we *do* leave, we'll probably never see these lands again."

Jacqueline jammed her shovel into the soil upright and turned to take in the view with Sabine. "That is a very good point. Hard to imagine, though. I mean, even after everything we've seen and how far we've come with Michael—the different countries and monsters—the thought of leaving this planet..." Her voice trailed off. "*Mind-blowing,*" she added after a moment.

Mark's voice broke their rapport. "Hey, you two! I know I have vamp-strength and all, but if I'm the only one digging this is gonna take a hell of a lot longer. And we're only on the first one. After this we've got another ten to go!"

Yuko and Eve were working on the other side of the nine-foot circle they'd traced around where the loot was.

Yuko called to Mark, "Remember what I explained about just digging one hole?"

"Yeah," he groaned, picking up his shovel again.

Eve chuckled. "You're trying to teach a tech-head vampire about Zen presence."

Yuko sniggered and replied in a hushed voice, "I thought it might help."

Eve continued digging, chuckling quietly. "You thought you'd amuse yourself."

Yuko put on her best earnest expression. "No, truly. I mean, it's how I get through mundane stuff, and it's good practice—to get really present and just work on the one thing you're doing right now. See?" She exaggerated her movement with the shovel. "I'm pulling out this one shovelful now." She tipped it onto the pile and turned back to the hole. "And this one, right now."

Eve did her best simulation of an eye roll.

"Presence!" Yuko declared.

Eve's chuckles subsided. "I suppose that's one way to keep your mind off Inspector Hottie."

Yuko's humor dissipated.

Eve noticed the change. "I'm sorry. I didn't mean to upset you."

Yuko shook her head. "You didn't. It's fine."

The two dug in silence for a few minutes.

"You know, if we end up getting this ship together and leaving you should probably at least let him know…so he doesn't wait his whole life for you."

Yuko didn't respond.

"Or you could see if Michael will let you bring him with you," she added.

Yuko flushed and wiped her face with the back of one hand. "I'll think about it," she muttered.

The humor returned to Eve's voice. "I'm sure he'd be very pleased to hear from you!" she added, almost teasing Yuko now.

Yuko's complexion was redder than the exertion could explain. "Stop it!" she said, trying to withhold a smile.

Eve changed the subject, glad she had at least made her point.

"Do you feel that?" Jacqueline asked as quietly as she could. She knew everyone with enhancements would hear her.

Yuko stopped digging suddenly, her eyes darting around them.

Mark stilled too, and Sabine's right hand hovered over her sidearm, although her left hand remained on the shovel.

Jacqueline sniffed the air. "I don't think we're alone."

The party stilled, scanning the area for any signs of movement.

There was nothing.

A few minutes later Sabine started digging again. "Probably just coyotes," she muttered.

Jacqueline returned to digging, too. "Yeah. Probably," she agreed, but she kept her senses tuned to their surroundings...just in case.

Near Site One, China

"Shit! Falling back, sir!" the soldier hissed into his comm unit as he elbow-crawled backward from the mound, keeping out of sight.

Once he reached the rest of the platoon, he slotted in next to their team leader.

"There are five," he reported. "Likely all enhanced, the way they're moving that earth."

The team leader nodded, his eyes fixed to his binoculars, scanning the summit of the mound for any signs they had been followed.

"They must have caught a whiff of me or something," the soldier continued. "They're alert now. They know we're here."

The team leader sighed, lowering the binoculars. He

scratched his face as he thought, and a moment later he made a decision.

He gave the hand signal for them to fall back. If they knew they were coming, they'd lost their advantage.

And if they were indeed enhanced, they'd need more than just the ten men he had right now.

He tapped a message to his commanding officer.

TARGETS AT LOCATION. THEY WON'T BE HERE MUCH LONGER. NEED REINFORCEMENTS AT NEXT LOCATION. ALL FIVE ENHANCED.

He punched **SEND**.

Quickly and quietly he followed his team, secretly relieved he had a legitimate reason to back away for now. After all, he'd heard stories about the monsters his comrades had fought over the years under Feng Cheng in defense of the crates, and while he wanted to perform his duty, he really didn't want to die.

Lanzhou Region, China

Commander Benjiro sat quietly in his makeshift office somewhere in the Chinese countryside. His satellite connection had gone silent for a few moments as the last dish slipped out of range and the replacement came online. His screens fuzzed with the black and white snow of an untended feed.

He used these moment to contemplate the details of the mission, weigh the odds, and ensure they were fulfilling their key outcomes. His success, he often told his trainees, was due to these moments of reflection.

The screens spluttered as they came back online. He

could see the helmet cams of his team at the active location. Nothing exciting...just more movement than before from the camera end, and a different horizon.

A message popped across the screen.

TARGETS AT LOCATION. THEY WON'T BE HERE MUCH LONGER. NEED REINFORCEMENTS AT NEXT LOCATION. ALL FIVE ENHANCED.

He paused, taking his hand away from his mouse.

This was not good.

He had expected one enhanced—the Diplomat—and maybe the android, but five?

This wasn't the deal.

He thought hard before he made a move. He was going to have to consult with Raiden on this.

And then there was the question of reinforcements. That was an accurate assessment on behalf of the team leader, Jon-joe. A good man. He cared about his men and about the job. He'd known him since even before this had become Chang Feng's operation.

His mind wandered to the crime scene photos of Feng's execution in the embassy. The blood spilled over the carpets and lush furnishings and the image of the executed emperor nearby were still etched heavily in his mind's eye.

He almost shuddered, but composed himself when he remembered he had subordinates at desks nearby. The sounds of the small camp came back to his awareness.

He made a fast assessment. If there were five enhanced personnel digging up the first site, it shouldn't take them much longer.

He leaned forward to his keyboard.

SENDING REINFORCEMENTS TO NEXT LOCA-TION. MAPPING YOUR TRAJ. BE SAFE.

He tapped **SEND**.

He looked up and beckoned for one of the sergeants to come over to him. The commander whispered orders to him, and the young soldier nodded his understanding before scuttling out of the tent.

Benjiro sighed and sat back. He should definitely let Raiden know, although there was no real hurry. He had it handled.

He reached into the drawer in the temporary foldout desk and retrieved a pack of cigarettes. After pulling one out, he scrambled for his Zippo in his cargo pants pocket.

He lit the cigarette and inhaled long and hard, his eyes focused into the distance as if it were the future and he was pulling the necessary information back.

Helping him plan the assault.

Undisclosed Location, Tokyo, Japan

Kuro sat quietly working on his sleek MCZ-book laptop. Being wired to a proprietary protocol allowed him to securely access the web from any location.

It had been one of the compelling reasons to bring Raiden onboard. Not so much to develop the protocol, which was already in hand, but to ensure that it was unhackable. That had been worth cutting Raiden in on their plans.

Raiden worked on the other side of the room, his foot tapping to the rhythm of the music blaring through his headphones. He was oblivious to the outside world.

The outside world trying to concentrate in the same room with him.

Kuro sighed, reminding himself of the patience he was trying to cultivate in order to be all he could be. He turned his eyes back to his screen.

Raiden's foot suddenly stopped tapping.

Finally.

Something had come in on his ops channel, no doubt.

Raiden scanned the communications window on his screen.

It was from Benjiro. Raiden read it once, twice…then a third time. "Son of a bitch!" he hissed, taking his headphones off.

"What is it?" Kuro called, interpreting the removal of the headphones as a sign he wanted to engage.

Raiden spun to him, jerking a thumb at his laptop. "Turns out those chickenshit Chinese soldiers don't want to engage. They're demanding reinforcements, and that means more money."

Kuro straightened his posture on the couch. "Or it means that they have an idea of what they're going up against now."

Raiden didn't respond. He was busy pounding on the keys.

I'LL PAY FOR THE MEN BUT NOTHING MORE. WHEN WE AGREED ON YOUR PRICE THE RISK WAS ALREADY FACTORED IN.

He punched **SEND**.

His fingers hovered over the keys like a tiger waiting in the trees to drop on an unsuspecting target.

Raiden started typing again and a sneer crept across his lips.

I WOULD ADVISE AGAINST TRYING TO CHANGE OUR AGREEMENT. IT WOULD END UP MOST UNSATISFACTORILY FOR YOU.

He hesitated for the briefest of moments, then hit **SEND** again.

He leaned back in his chair and exhaled, then quietly steepled his fingers and started giving a low guttural rumbling laugh. "Mwuhahahahaaa…" He turned slowly in his chair to face the spartan room.

Kuro glanced up again, one eyebrow raised.

Raiden, suddenly embarrassed, coughed. "Sorry. I…er…just always wanted to do that, but since I've never run my own operation, it just never felt right."

Kuro nodded once. "And now?"

Raiden nodded. "Hell yeah, *now* it feels right!" he answered, grinning before turning back around.

Overconfidence will drown you in the sea of reality.

The words sprang into Kuro's mind like a strategic warning. He shook his head.

There was little point in trying to temper the egocentric mind of youth. He would be better off saving his breath and letting the operation kick the man's ass. Maybe then Raiden would be willing to ask others for counsel in this and the other projects he had running.

CHAPTER FOUR

<u>Undisclosed Location Somewhere in the Takla Makan Desert, China</u>

"Ughhhhhhh!" Mark grunted as he and Yuko pulled the crate another five feet. "You've got to be kidding me! There isn't a material on this planet that could weigh this much in such a small container!"

Sabine was observing, having already taken her turn at pulling the monstrously weighty crate from the bottom of the ten-foot hole they had spent the afternoon digging. "You do remember the part about this stuff being from another planet, right?" she teased, regaining her strength with each minute she rested.

Jacqueline wandered up, having deposited the shovels in the box. "Aww, is Marky-Warky having to do some work that is more physical than playing with computers?"

Even Eve chuckled at the pair.

Yuko was silent as she exerted her strength. After another five feet, the pair stopped to catch their breath.

"All I'm saying is that it's very convenient that Mr.

ArchAngel is off mind-reading engineers while we're out here busting our balls," Mark replied.

The ladies stared at him and he checked himself, "I mean... Busting a gut, that is."

Jacqueline slapped his shoulder. "Move, vamp-boy. Let me try."

Yuko heaved with her and they hauled the crate the last five feet into the black box.

The group cheered, albeit in a muted way rather than in outright celebration.

"Two down, nine to go!" Sabine exclaimed, summing up the overall mood.

Mark dramatically collapsed on the ground.

Jacqueline sniffed the air and her body tensed in readiness.

Sabine unconsciously fixed her eyes on the horizon. Already her guns were unholstered, safeties off.

Yuko glanced at Eve. It was almost as if they had communicated with eye contact. Eve dodged into the cabin and emerged with her missile launcher, her arm already adapting to accommodate it.

Mark was the last one to cotton to what was happening. His vamp ears pricked up when he heard the distant shuffle of cloth against cloth and boots against sand, and then there was a distant hum of a chopper.

The team's minds screamed, *AMBUSH!*

Eve spoke quietly. "Ok people, this is it. The same people we sensed earlier, except there are more of them. Our primary goal is to protect the cargo. Oh yeah, and don't die. Michael wouldn't like that."

She caught Sabine's eye, and was going to add something about Akio, but the first of the soldiers came over the mound in the distance.

Yuko had positioned herself for a fight, her sword at the ready, but after seeing the distance the enemy had to cover before they got within sword's length she dropped her arms.

Sabine grinned. "I got this," she told them, zoning out. She felt the wind, and could hear the clothes scrape against the leaves and preternaturally see where the next person was without having a clue why.

Gently and gracefully she squeezed the triggers on her Jean Dukes, almost dancing with each shot as the troops started running toward them to engage.

Body after body crumpled like paper dolls in the wind.

Yuko turned to Jacqueline with an eyebrow raised. "Guess we were worried for no reason."

Mark dusted the sand out of his hair from when he had dropped to the ground and chuckled. "No kidding."

Sabine stopped firing, and the sound of the chopper suddenly turned from a hum to a roar as it appeared from another direction.

It was above them in moments.

"Protect the cargo!" Yuko ordered, her sword out in front of her once more. She watched uniformed bodies fast-rope from the chopper to the ground.

Sabine could make a few shots, but the trees blocked much of her view in that direction.

Within moments there were numerous soldiers with guns and knives fighting fists and fangs with the group.

Eve had moved away from the chopper to be able to angle her launcher correctly, and before all the men were safely on the ground she sent her first missile. The chopper swerved to avoid it and was clipped, sending it spinning.

Yuko sliced through a torso before turning to her. "Something wrong with your aim?"

Eve chuckled. "My hand slipped!" she admitted before popping off a second small missile which tore straight through the body of the machine, tossing it backward like a ball of crumpled paper into a trash can.

Yuko ducked the swipe of a knife-wielding soldier and followed the motion with a slice which cut through him from the chest upwards. "That second shot was much better," she called to the very satisfied-looking Eve.

Twice Mark had been pushed to the side by his girlfriend, her snarls ripping toward soldiers attacking him.

Twice she had been hit by bullets in his place, her howls of pain quickly followed by men screaming as a male-sun walking vampire shredded their bodies in his anger, ending their lives.

Sabine had been popping bullets into anything she could see that was coming from the chopper, but now that it was gone she turned her pistols on the crowd, deftly spotting the opponents who were narrowing in on her friends.

Sabine was in her zone. She turned to the right, shooting a man who had been thrown by Jacqueline in the head, which exploded before his body landed twenty feet away. Continuing her turn, she shot another in the leg and his gun jerked up, the bullet uselessly hitting some leaves before Yuko's sword sliced through his neck.

Completing her turn, she waited the barest of moments before squeezing her trigger. The chest of a mercenary exploded and her bullet exited the first man to hit another fifteen feet behind him in the neck, taking out a chunk of flesh the size of a hand.

It took somewhere between seven and fifteen seconds before the only things breathing—if not entirely living by traditional measures—were the five who had been digging up the crates.

Yuko gazed at the carnage and sighed, carefully wiping her blade on the nearest body. "We probably should clear up this mess, but I for one am too tired." She glanced at the others. "What say we just finish packing up and get out of here?"

By the time she'd finished her sentence the crew had gathered the rest of their equipment and were loading it into the black box.

Yuko smiled, satisfied. *Nothing like the mundane tasks to motivate movement in the troops,* she mused, stepping onboard and pulling the door closed behind her.

She was kind of getting used to having a larger team.

Lanzhou Region, China

Cigarette smoke hung in the air, visible only where the daylight entered the tent and directly under the artificial lights illuminating the workstations.

Crushed cigarette butts lay on the dried grass around the righthand side of the commander's chair.

"Sir, we've lost contact."

Benjiro leaned forward to retrieve the last cancer-stick from the beaten-up pack and nodded, dismissing the messenger.

He paused, looking at the cigarette. Instead of putting it into his mouth, he placed it back on the desk in front of him and shuffled his chair closer to his keyboard.

This couldn't wait.

UPDATE. ALL 30 TROOPS AND CHOPPER TAKEN OUT. AWAITING FURTHER INSTRUCTION.

He hit **SEND.**

He sat back, eyes falling to the cigarette again. If this was going to continue, he figured he'd need that hit more later than right now.

He tried to still his mind. He could sense the chatter amongst his men increasing, though they'd never comment to him directly. He glanced at them, noticing one in the huddle around the work station looking at him . The soldier quickly gazed back down at the screen, pretending to be absorbed in a conversation about the work.

Benjiro knew better.

He'd been in their position many a time when he was a younger man. Wondering if he was going to be next, wondering how his teammates had been taken out by an enemy who had very little in the way of manpower or artillery.

It was one of the things that had led him to his current position. Fear.

The computer icon blipped, displaying a new message.

ALL IS NOT LOST...

The cursor blinked at the end of the ellipsis.

Benjiro waited, subconsciously reaching for the cigarette and putting it between his lips.

COMM SIGNAL STILL ACTIVE. MEN DEAD, BUT TECH OK. ONE TRACKER PLACED AS PLANNED.

HAS BEEN ACTIVATED. TRACKING TARGETS NOW. WILL SHARE FREQUENCY IN A MO.

Benjiro waited, reading and re-reading the message. His thoughts were interrupted by a flurry of quiet activity at the other console. One of the soldiers hurried over to him.

"Sir, they've activated Phase Two. We've just received the signal and we're tracking them now. If all goes well, we'll be able to triangulate their next location within the hour. So far it looks like they're moving inland."

Benjiro nodded, and the sergeant went away.

A new message had appeared on his screen.

TRACK THEM. HAVE NEXT TEAM IN PLACE FOR NEXT LOCATION. WE TRY AGAIN.

Benjiro lit the cigarette, knowing that he had no choice. He was going to have to sacrifice another thirty lives on a mission where they really didn't stand a chance. He leaned forward and sent the confirmation before sitting back and looking off into space.

<u>Tokyo, Japan</u>

Michael watched as the next candidate crossed the floor. She bowed to Akio and reached over to shake Michael's hand. "Hello," she started when Akio waved to the chair. "I'm Yuko."

God, no! Michael told Akio immediately. *Can you imagine what would happen if we had two Yukos on our team?*

"Please, take a seat," Akio asked. "This will be a very short conversation about the skills you suggest you have, and your honesty."

You are telling me that even if she is fully capable you would remove her from consideration since she has the same name as Yuko?

Absolutely, no question, Michael replied. *I can already hear the bitching if we had two with the same name. The help would crucify me.* Michael thought about that for a second. *No pun intended.*

Just for having two Yukos?

Imagine if you will, Michael started, *that someone says, "Yuko told me to take this gadget down to Sublevel Six." Now, an easy—and very subtle—mind-read would confirm she is telling the truth. The problem—*

Would be this *Yuko was actually the one who gave the order.* Akio nodded his head ever so slightly. *I understand.*

The woman stared at the two men, who had yet to say anything although they had smiles plastered on their faces. "One moment," the Japanese man said and turned to her.

Would it help to know, Akio continued as he reviewed the information on this applicant, *that she goes by "Hideko?"*

Well, if she wasn't a plant by a man named Raiden, then probably. Michael stood up. *Why is it always the pretty ones? Doesn't anyone have any sense around here? I've met many smart people who are not necessarily attractive, and they all go under the radar. It's almost a slap in the face to assume I wouldn't presume that any attractive applicant wasn't a spy.*

You are very cynical already, Akio mused.

It doesn't change the accuracy of my statement, or the reality that she is a plant.

Or that you have now identified someone we can take down?

Well, it's small recompense for my butt having gone to sleep sitting on these old plastic chairs.

Akio shrugged. *Most of the available chairs I could grab were left over from government buildings, and I figured the humans would wish to leave quickly if we used them. It worked out well with the last applicant.* Akio tried to smile, and it almost looked right. *I figured our nanocytes would protect us.*

From gunshots, yes, Michael replied with an annoyed look on his face. *But not from government chairs hurting my ass.* He stood up. "I'll let the next person know they can come in, and then I'll take the young lady to HR."

What HR? Akio asked.

Me, Michael replied. *I wear many hats.*

You are just happy to get out of these interviews for a moment.

Moment? Michael replied, a smile touching his lips. *This might take me hours.*

When Bethany Anne gets here I'll have to admit it took you a long time to interrogate her.

He shook his head. *Or it might be very quick. Whoever taught you to loosen up should have their ass kicked.*

Akio just chuckled. Their candidate's eyes were wide in shock, which turned to fear when Michael stood up since his eyes were glowing red.

"You will come with me," he told her.

CHAPTER FIVE

Tokyo, Japan

Akio stood outside the building they were using to interview subjects, watching Michael as he sent mental commands to the male and female next to him.

"Eve?" he called, waiting for her to answer the comm signal.

"Here," she replied. "We will soon be heading back to the warehouse for the Clan's material."

"I need you to track down a name on the dark web. Is this possible?"

Eve's voice, if it *could* sound cocky, sounded that way now to Akio. "You know the dark web is just another name for *my* house, yes? No one comes into my house without me knowing who they are."

"Good to know," Akio replied. "I need to find out who TigerDragon_NV is, since he has visited your house, and locate him. I have two additional names you can use to narrow the communications which happened in your house, and request you deliver to me an address to visit. I do not believe this person will ever visit your house again."

"Am I sensing an attitude? Not that I mind, of course, but I need to know. Is it one of annoyance, or of challenge?" the android asked. Akio could tell he was receiving only a small portion of her analytical capability as she continued the discussion.

He waited for Eve patiently as Michael finished with the two moles and sent them on their way. Soon enough, Michael walked back in his direction with his lips pressed in a grim line.

The Dark Messiah was pissed.

"Anytime now would be good, Eve." Akio turned his attention back to the conversation.

"Just…one…more…moment," she replied, then, "Got it!"

Akio's tablet beeped and he tilted it to examine a map with a location that was out of the city noted. "He is smart, but uses a very similar typing pattern. I have found five other aliases he has used when visiting my house," she said as Akio smirked. "One of those aliases was used to connect to the dark web just three minutes ago after going dark in Tokyo an hour and a half ago."

Michael was standing with Akio, his attention focused outward and his hands clasped together behind his back.

"I understand. Please bring my ship down here." He touched a point on the map. "We will be at the top of the building within five minutes."

"It will happen, Akio," Eve replied. "Just be aware that clouds will block my view of the building top within ten minutes should Michael choose to school another mouthy person and you two fail to get there in your projected time."

Akio smirked, his eyes flitting to Michael. "Understood, She-Who-Can-See-All."

The two disconnected. "This way," Akio told the Arch-Angel as he turned toward the street.

"What did Eve say?" Michael asked. "What did she see?"

"Nothing special," Akio answered, "but she needs us to be on top of a nearby building within the next ten minutes or the clouds will block her view."

Michael followed him, his eyes watching everyone around them.

Always watching.

Farthest Western Edge of Takla Makan Desert

Eve completed a final scan of the grounds. "That's everything," she announced to Yuko.

Jacqueline and Mark had just finished heaving the last crate into the black box. "Thank goodness for that!" Mark grunted, pushing it farther into the cabin with one last effort.

Jacqueline jumped over it and hopped out again. "You're telling me! I think my nanocytes have decided to grow muscles on top of my muscles. Feel!" She flexed her arm and nodded to Yuko, encouraging her to feel.

Sabine chuckled. "You Americans! You're *soooo* funny."

Mark joined in the laughter until a quick glare from Jacqueline caused his merriment to change to a coughing fit.

Jacqueline smiled. "Well, Frenchy, or should I say, 'Frog—'"

Yuko held her hand up. "Come on, Jacqueline. It's been a long week. Let's get this last one back to the hangar and find out when our engineers will be arriving. Then maybe you all can go and blow off some steam somewhere...without tearing each other apart."

Sabine smiled innocently.

Jacqueline narrowed her eyes, then avoided all eye contact.

She didn't dislike Sabine. She was just hot and irritated, and Sabine hardly even seemed to break a sweat in the heat.

Next to the Frenchwoman—with her slim waist and cute accent—she felt like a bumbling werewolf...and was just a little sensitive about having other females laughing with her boyfriend.

Sabine had wandered off, collecting the pieces of equipment and the ropes they'd been using. Jacqueline was too exhausted to even walk another fifty yards, so she stepped back into the cabin and laid down on the floor until the others were ready.

Mark helped gather the shovels, and within a short time the team—their routine down by now—were ready for takeoff.

Yuko scanned the horizon one last time just to be sure. "Good to not be leaving another crimson crime scene," she called to Eve.

"Agreed. Nothing on radar, either."

Yuko slowly closed the door. "Can't believe anyone

would only send one team after us though." She joined Eve at the computer terminals.

Eve stopped her checks. "You think they'll come again, even though we've switched locations?"

Yuko sighed. "I have to believe they will. If what Akio saw was accurate, we're probably still being tracked somehow."

Eve frowned. "But he neutralized that threat."

Yuko tilted her head. "I sure hope so."

The black box lifted gently from the ground, and in no time at all was nothing but a speck in the sky.

Stuck to its underside, undetectable to most readers, a lone device emitted the slightest of signals, blipping away on an unused frequency.

The frequency was picked up by a geostationary satellite and the signal forwarded to a server just off the coast of China, then relayed through a number of proxies in Japan and bounced through a hub station, only to be converted into a new protocol which five whole seconds later appeared on the screen in China.

Lanzhou Region, China

"Sir, looks like they're on the move again," the soldier reported from the second console.

Benjiro had been deep in thought, but he straightened up and took a breath before asking, "Where now?"

"Back to the hangar, sir," the soldier replied. "Sir, that's all eleven boxes now."

The other soldiers gathered quietly around the console and waited expectantly for the order. For a whole week they'd been excused from meeting the fate of the first team, but every one of them knew the hour was fast approaching. Eventually they would all have to face the monsters who had dug up these assets from their desolate land.

"Very good, Sergeant," Benjiro responded. "Make the team ready. We hit the hangar at nightfall."

The company exploded into a very quiet flurry of nervous activity.

Finally, they had their orders.

The commander leaned forward, placing his fingers over the keyboard to report their progress. Raiden should be pleased, at least. Soon he'd have all the pieces without having had to hire anyone to go dig them up.

Benjiro started typing his message.

Undisclosed location, Tokyo, Japan

"*Kuso kuso kuso!*" Raiden spat, pounding the keys harder to try to rectify the situation.

Kuro looked up from across the apartment. "What is it?"

"Comms just went dead," he answered, disgusted.

Kuro sighed. Raiden was a techie; a developer of code, not assets. He stood up and wandered across the bare floorboards to the computer setup. "Whose comms?"

Raiden stopped typing. "Both science moles. The connections are gone. Dead, as if the devices were obliterated."

Kuro stood still, quietly evaluating the situation. After a few moments he said, "And you think it was the Diplomat in China?"

Raiden scratched his head, his eyes flicking from one screen to another. "I don't *think* so," he replied sarcastically, "I'm sure of it. Benjiro said he spied a Japanese female with an android sidekick on-site at one of his locations."

"Hmm. So, if the Diplomat is not the one interviewing the recruits, who is?" he asked Raiden.

Raiden paused a moment, then pulled up a file. "Here." He pointed to the screen. "This is an image of one of the interviewers one candidate was able to send me before he went in for his interview."

The picture on the screen showed a Japanese man poking his head round a door.

"Do we know who that is?" Kuro asked.

Raiden didn't answer. Instead he analyzed it against images sent by assets over the last few weeks.

The program pinged a response almost immediately.

"*Kuso*." He cursed once more when he saw the match.

Kuro took a very deep breath after he read the name. "Agreed," he answered finally.

The image matched one of the destroyers.

Kuro glanced down at Raiden. "You know what this means?"

Raiden shook his head.

"It means they likely had their minds read, and that was how they were discovered. Tell me, did you ever meet with them?"

Raiden shook his head. "Of course not," he said, too afraid to be indignant.

Kuro pressed the point. "Did they know who you were? How did you meet them?"

"On the dark web. They only know my screen name," Raiden replied.

Kuro's face was grave, his lips compressed. "It may be enough. They'll be able to track you down, especially if they're working with the Diplomat and her android. They have a special way of finding out anything they need to know if it's hooked up to technology. That's why they've remained so elusive." He lowered his voice. "And why *we've* historically been very careful about approaching them."

Raiden's eyes filled with concern—or maybe it was terror. "You mean to say I'm possibly a dead man walking?"

Kuro nodded his head once, his eyes going from the picture to Raiden and back. "I'm sorry, yes," he confirmed. "I recommend you go into hiding and disappear. Off-grid. No computers. No tech. No forwarding address."

Raiden stared into space for a moment.

"You don't seem to get the urgency of this. I meant right *now!*" he said, his voice conveying his sudden anxiety.

And with that Kuro strode back across the room, collected his laptop, and started pushing it into its case as if he meant to leave.

Then he stopped, thinking.

As if changing his mind, he dropped the case back onto the sofa and took the laptop into the kitchen. Raiden could hear plastic snapping and breaking, and then the microwave turning on.

Then small pops and explosions.

And an awful smell of toxic chemicals.

Kuro emerged, threw his jacket on, and strode toward the door. He stopped next to Raiden and faced him. "It's been an honor working with you. I hope we both survive this, though I doubt we will. I wish you luck."

He hurriedly embraced his friend and disappeared out the door, closing it softly behind him.

Raiden glanced at the laptop case on the sofa, then at the smoke emanating from the kitchen, which lingered in the air and cast patterns as it caught the sunlight. For Kuro to do that to his laptop—which contained his life and business operations, the action presumably taken because it had been on this network—was extreme.

Raiden left everything including his phone where it was and exited the building as fast as he could.

Unfortunately, Raiden couldn't live without tech in his life.

CHAPTER SIX

<u>Japan, Mount Fuji in the distance</u>

"Where the hell are we?" Michael whispered to Akio as they stood under the trees looking at Tokyo with its little lights zipping around the city in the air. "They look like Christmas lights at times."

"There is Fuji-san," Akio pointed to the southwest, and of course there is Tokyo, about thirty of your miles in almost the opposite direction. He looked down at his tablet and pointed north. "The lab is about five minutes that direction in your Myst."

Michael pulled off his hat and ran his hand through the stubble of his hair before putting it back on. "And you say that Eve uncovered evidence of nanocyte experiments?"

"*Hai*," Akio admitted. "The young lady had no knowledge of their security?"

"Nope," Michael replied. "She was hired for her science knowledge and her looks." Michael sighed as the two of them started walking toward the building. "At this age, it becomes laughable what some people use to try to cloud the minds of those they are attacking." Michael's eyes flicked to Akio. "And good job not mentioning the Duke and the Hadron Collider."

Akio shrugged, leaving the rest unsaid. "So, go in as Myst, check it out, and deal with the results?"

"I believe that will do the job." Michael switched to Myst, grabbed Akio, and sped in the direction of the lab. *Do you wish to come inside, or stay outside and catch any rats trying to leave the boat?*

I'll play catch this time, Akio replied. *I'm not quite as bombproof as you are, and I'd hate to get wiped out at the very end.*

Bethany Anne would have a few choice words for me if I lost you before she got back.

And more for me if you *die, so please don't.* Akio chuckled. *Eve said there were lower levels.*

Akio could hear Michael's sigh. *Of course there are.*

Michael deposited Akio two blocks from the three-story white concrete building, which gleamed in the reflected moonlight. Akio noticed there were windows only on the top floor as he moved into the darker shadows, working his way toward the north side of the building.

One nice thing about secure buildings was their small number of entrances and exits.

Michael passed the north-side security gate and checked on the guard there. His mind was active, but Michael could discern no knowledge of anything inside the building.

It took him a few minutes to circle the lab, but he finally found a vent pipe he could use to enter.

He'd didn't want to go in the most obvious way and suffer even remotely what he had back in Europe. William was dead now, but the pain of keeping himself together in the Hadron Collider was still fresh in his mind.

Caution was now his...well, not his middle name, but perhaps his cousin's name. Either way, he was going to be a bit more careful this time.

He came out of the pipe in a restroom on the second floor. He discovered as he flitted through the place there were only three people on this floor: one security guard and two computer personnel. One was playing a game system as they sat in front of a bank of monitors watching some screens.

Or rather, Michael noted, not watching them.

Michael read the man's thoughts and frowned. After diving deeper into his memories, he floated back to the security guard and burrowed deeply, lifting memories from months back.

Then from over a year ago.

Releasing the mind, he felt above him in the building and then below. There wasn't anyone above him, and as far as he could tell the programmer on this floor was ignorant of what was below-ground. Considering the research focus, Michael guessed many of those who worked here had no idea that there were two companies intertwined at this location.

The company on top, and the company under the ground.

Michael solidified behind the security guard, his three-inch-long nails dagger-sharp, and grabbed the top of the man's head.

He flexed his fingers and the nails impaled the man's skull. Michael bent down closer to the man, whose body was flailing under the ArchAngel's arm. "You have seen the pain of others. You watched them as they begged to be released from the experiments. Some died as you played your games or watched in fascination!"

Michael clenched his fist and the body stopped thrashing. "Now, no one is here to watch you jerk around or hear you beg for your life." Michael wiped his hand on the guard's shirt. "As you did not save others, no one was here to save you," he said as he changed back to Myst and headed for a small area he could slip into. He made it to the other side of the cement wall, and into the elevator shaft.

Michael mentally called as he drifted to the first underground level, *Akio?*

Hai?

Read the minds of those you can see. If they work for the research department above, let them go. Those who work for the research labs below-ground need to be eradicated. They are working on Wechselbalg, and before that brought a vampire in here before who died. They're using them for the nanocyte research, trying to see if they can use the blood to change others.

Like the blood-baggers in England?

Not exactly. Michael thought for a moment, pulling out the memories of the now-dead guard. *More like seeing what else they can make. I'm sure they have some knowledge of the enhancement to humans, but it seems like they are being very tentative with humans so far. They are using animals for test subjects. Well,* Michael amended, *they are tentative in testing pure humans. Those with nanocytes are nothing to these people.*

Michael sent over a few images he had pulled from the guard.

We will be killing them all?

And burning what we can't kill, Michael agreed.

Michael Mysted through the crack between the elevator doors and floated down the hallway, wishing there were more people here during the night shift. If there had been, more of those who deserved what was coming would have been here to receive it.

In the first corner office Michael found one mind which made him smile.

BINGO!

Raiden had pushed his small laptop to the side of his desk and was using his keyboard, reviewing the information on his dual-monitor setup. Kuro had given him too much to think about. This time the failure wouldn't mean hacked code, but that his blood would be spilled everywhere.

He had covered his tracks.

At least he hoped he had covered his tracks.

This was his most secure site. Few knew of it, and fewer still knew of the underground work they did here. His own partners understood very little of what he was capable of doing. To them he was just a code-head.

But for those who understood, the human genome was just the code for the human body, and the aliens who placed the advanced nanocytes in the werewolves and the vampires had provided him with the hint he needed to write the ultimate program…

The human body.

He didn't doubt that the nanocytes were alien in nature. He *had* studied all the history he could get hold of, and Raiden had tracked down the different code bases as nearly as he could tell.

One he had named after TQB, and that was the vampires. Another he had labeled "W" for the Werewolves and the last was simply "C" for the cats, or the Sacred Clan. As near as he could tell from researching the Clan, they weren't connected to the werewolves at all and certainly not with TQB.

Then there were the rumored Russian bears, but even *he'd* had problems finding out much about them. The one time he'd thought he had a good computer connection his hack had been slapped back so fast he was sure he had physically felt it.

The stupid Clan members were too damned close and he worked with some of them as well, so he didn't dare use any of them for experiments. He didn't even use any of the cats they turned for his experiments.

It had taken him eight long months to locate a mountain lion from the former Americas and get it shipped to him.

And she was *perfect*.

At just over eighty pounds she wasn't as large as she *could* get, but maybe that would change if he could get the nanocytes to work effectively. He had used up his vampire stock just two nights ago, and they were waiting for her latest injections to run through her system. Raiden wasn't going to allow any issues between the TQB nanocytes and the W nanocytes to kill his prized test subject.

He was checking her latest nanocyte count when he felt cold, as if a ghost had just brushed him.

"Ehhhh?" Raiden jerked to his left, then to his right to look for anything that might have touched him. He pushed his chair back, making sure to bang it against the credenza against the wall behind him to make sure nobody was there, either.

"Damn you, Kuro!" he spat before grabbing his headphones. The music would help him focus...or at least he hoped it would.

"You will work here until morning," a soft voice, like velvet over steel, whispered in his ear. *"I will be back for you!"* it finished, the words dissipating into the air and just touching his subconscious before leaving.

Raiden shivered once more, but had no idea why.

Michael checked out the first underground level and the second. The elevator stopped at the first level. Only stairs went down to the rest.

The first level held five people: Raiden, three security officers near Raiden's office, and a female who was cursing a lot while working in her own office on some sort of math program.

On the second there were three more security people

carrying bull-pup submachine guns like those above, and they also had ten-inch daggers strapped to their chest protectors. Michael counted three surgical rooms, one of which smelled as if it had been used in the last couple days and two that just smelled like antiseptic.

There were no workers on the second level.

He moved down the stairs to the bottom level and stopped for a moment to take in the cages of animals and seven humans. Six were male, and one was female.

The female was in the back of a cage, her eyes wide and a snarl on her lips as she watched two males in lab coats head toward her. Their attention was on a clipboard one was sharing with the other. The security guards followed the two of them, one wielding a shock-rod and a second a long staff with a loop at the end.

One would grab her by the neck, the other shock her.

Michael recognized the arc rod as being similar to the ones he'd messed with in New York.

A regular Wechselbalg wouldn't be able to handle the shock, that was for sure.

Hoping that no one else was watching the video cameras, Michael dropped out of the Myst right next to the door that led up to the second floor and locked it. He could hear screams behind him.

Then Michael broke off the knob.

***

Tanith growled low in her throat and her eyes flashed brownish-yellow as she watched the two scientists come toward her.

Each time they did this she'd fought them tooth and nail. Last time they had injected her with something that stopped her transformation but left her the rest of her Wechselbalg advantages in human state.

Unfortunately that damned shock-rod was sufficient to lay her out long enough for them to get the chokehold on her neck.

The first scientist came up to her cage. "Tanith, are you going to fight us?"

"Yesss," she hissed. "You dare touch us? You and your lackeys?" She tilted her head toward the security detail.

The scientist reached up to adjust his glasses, ignoring the five behind him. "They are no different than me or you. My boss just has more advantages than you."

"Why don't you wake up Gaku and Shiang and we shall see who has the advantage?"

The scientist shook his head, and stepped back. "Let it be recorded in the notes that I tried."

"You did, sir." The first guard, the one with the arc rod, came forward. "Step back, sir."

Tanith's eyes narrowed. He had always come into the cage before, so his smirk should have warned her that he had figured out a new way to…

"*AAAHHYYYEEE!*" she screamed when he touched the stick to the cage itself. The bars electrified her muscles, which spasmed. She fell toward the middle of the space, the tendrils of fire arcing through her body, but there was a moment of respite when he stopped shocking the cage.

Then he touched her shoulder with the rod, and she tasted the blood of her tongue as the spasms made what had happened before seem like someone had just been tickling her.

CHAPTER SEVEN

Japan, Mount Fuji in the distance

"We need her for these tests," the second scientist sniffed as Isami lifted the shock-rod off Tanith. His partner Goro stepped through the cage door and slipped the noose around her neck as her body convulsed.

"She can't kill us, either," Isami replied. "Dai is still in the hospital, and he will have only one eye for the rest of his life."

The six men turned in surprise as a deep laugh sounded in both their minds and their ears. "I wouldn't worry about *her* killing you."

A man in a black hat and long coat stood behind them, his eyes flaring red. "I am Death, and I've been charged with bringing you to Hell."

Isami pushed Choki out of the way and raised his arc rod, the angry spitting of the electricity sizzling in the silence. "Over our dead bodies!"

"That was the plan," he agreed.

"Who are you?" Isami asked as Choki and Zan stepped

to each side of him and brought their bullpup submachine guns up to their shoulders.

Michael's eyes flicked to the men with the guns trained on him. "I've had many names. Which one would you like?" he asked obligingly

"The one we should put on your tombstone," Isami answered, and shoving off his left foot he jumped forward, wielding the rod like a foil and reaching forward to spear the man.

His eyes widened in shock when the man caught the end with his right hand. "Hehehehe ," he laughed merrily as the electricity jumped between his eyes and the blue reflections of the sparks played in them.

A second later the rod suddenly dimmed, as if he'd pulled all its energy into himself. "It tickles," he told them. "Let me hand this back to you," he told Isami, and handed the now-dead rod back to him. "Where are my manners?" He smiled. "My name is Michael. 'The ArchAngel' to some, 'the Dark Messiah' to others. I believe I failed to give this back as well." The rod's energy fried the three security men in front of Michael as he passed it to them. Michael had to switch to Myst because two of the men fired spasmodically as their bodies jerked.

Michael reappeared behind the scientists and shoved them toward the three security guards, and they stumbled into the streams of bullets.

"That's one," Michael murmured as one of the scientist's bodies jerked when bullets stitched up his torso, blowing small chunks of flesh out the back.

The second scientist fell past both guards, the bullets missing him. "Pity, that." The last security guard had pulled the noose off the Wechselbalg and was trying to get it out of the cage. Michael moved forward and grabbed the end of the pole, yanking it out of his hands and slamming the cage door shut. "Stay there for a moment." Michael winked to the woman inside, who looked like she had control of her muscles again. "I'll kill you in a moment if she doesn't do it first," he told the man while nodding to the woman behind him.

The man reached for his knife but her foot slammed his face, bouncing the back of his head off the metal bars and causing him to lose focus.

Tanith daintily pulled the knife out of his fingers. "Let me return this to you," she said, as she slammed the knife into his skull, right above his ear.

Goro's body slid sideways and collapsed.

She watched as the man in the coat reached down and lifted one of the submachine guns, turning it to the side and cocking it. The second scientist was stumbling toward the exit when three bullets stitched up his spine, the last round entering the back of his neck and exiting right above his mouth.

"And that makes six." Michael turned around, tossing the gun on the dead security guard as he spoke to Tanith. "They don't make security guards like they used to."

Michael stepped up to the cage and unlocked it. "How do we wake your friends?"

Tanith pointed toward the wall. There was a grey desk with a cabinet next to it. "Inside the locked cabinet are shots. The blue-topped ones will wake them." She grimaced as she lifted the bloody lab coat. "He's got some keys here somewhere…"

She turned when she heard a loud *slam* to see that Michael had punched a hole in the cabinet door and simply ripped it off. A few boxes fell out as Michael looked around and then reached in and pulled out two syringes, their tops blue. He turned to her, lifting them. "These?"

She nodded.

He walked over to her and held them out. "Wake them," he told her and continued past her. "I've got to prepare this place."

She accepted the syringes and turned to go to Gaku's and Shiang's cages, not happy to be ordered but really not wanting to piss off her liberator either.

She could flip him off once they were outside.

"If you flip me off," he said from the far side of the room as he continued opening drawers and slamming them shut, "I will rip your finger completely off and shove it up your ass."

Ok, maybe she would just wake up Shiang and Gaku and get the hell out of here.

"That is a much better plan," he told her as she unlocked Gaku's cage and stepped in, bending down to give him the shot.

Stepping out, she did the same for Shiang.

He walked up with a pile of paper and a lighter in his hands.

Gaku was walking as if in a daze and she was supporting Shiang, his arm over her shoulders. "What are you going to do?"

"Burn this place," Michael answered. "I could do it another way, but I'm feeling the need to be an old-fashioned pyromaniac." He reached over, placing a hand on

Shiang's shoulder. "One second." He willed energy into the man's body.

"What are you doing?" Tanith whispered. "I feel that!"

Shiang came out of his stupor as Michael did the same for Gaku. "Don't push anything yet. The nanocytes will help you, but it will still take a little while." He walked up to the door, grabbing the handle and twisting.

The damned handle broke off in his hand, leaving a two-inch hole in the door—which was still locked. "Well." He stared at the handle in his hand, and then the hole in the door. "Shit," he muttered as he tossed the handle to the side. "Ok." He set the paper and the lighter on a desk to the side. "This is going to feel weird, but I've got this."

He disappeared.

Tanith drew in a breath when the vampire disappeared, and then…

Keep quiet! a voice said inside her head. *You are almost clear.*

Soon enough, Tanith, Gaku and Shiang appeared on the other side of the door. They checked their bodies and looked at each other in shock.

"What just happened?" Shiang asked.

They heard a voice from inside the room. "I pulled you out of there using a special ability I have. I've just got to start this fire…" The three Wechselbalg smelled the paper go up.

"What about Demon?" Tanith asked.

"Who?" Michael replied, his surprise evident.

Me, a voice called in Michael's mind.

He peered into the back corner of the large room. "Who's that?" Michael asked.

"The mountain lion!" Tanith answered, her voice coming through the hole.

Of course. Michael pressed his lips together, switched to Myst, and headed to where he could feel the other body.

He found the mountain lion in a sealed glass cage and solidified outside it. "Damned airtight shit," he muttered, then looked at the mountain lion, who was staring back at him in curiosity, "You might want to move to the far corner," he said, and was surprised when the cat jumped to the farthest corner in the cage.

Michael figured there had to be an air inlet somewhere, but he wasn't going to spend the time to find it.

That is really hard to break. I've tried, the soft voice told him. Raising an eyebrow in the cat's direction, he smiled. "You're smart," Michael muttered as he slammed his fist into the glass, shattering it, "but you need to know your limits."

Michael reached up to knock some of the larger pieces out of the window and smiled at the mountain lion, who was still watching him. He clapped his hands together twice. "Come here!"

Demon could smell the smoke, but she eyed the man and mentally shrugged.

What did she have to lose? She was heavy, and if nothing else he would probably soften her fall.

She jumped over the broken glass and had just touched the man's chest when he disappeared.

Her eyes opened in surprise as she disappeared as well.

Lanzhou Region, China

Benjiro glanced down at his handheld. It had been at least forty minutes since his last message, and still no response from Raiden.

The soldiers around him had already dismantled the tent and loaded all their tech onto the chopper. He would get the all-clear for departure before much longer.

He logged into the handheld again, hoping to dislodge any stuck messages.

Nothing.

He felt the anxiety in the pit of his stomach. He'd been in tense situations before. Combat situations, even. Nothing compared to this, though. This was their whole *raison d'etre*. It was the reason he had stayed in the service as a career officer. He had been honored when he was selected for this team, but when Chang Feng was assassinated everything had seemed lost.

The locations. The leadership.

Raiden had given them new hope.

And now he wasn't responding.

The sunlight was starting to wane. He wasn't sure about attacking the hangar in darkness, especially without having surveyed the building in daylight. Sure, satellite images were useful, but they weren't the same as doing a few loops and getting down on one's belly button with sights to see what they were dealing with.

He wandered away from the remains of the camp to think.

It wasn't like Raiden to be out of communication even for five minutes. He would have thought the guy took his comm with him to take a shit.

But even if he was down, the mission was still in play.

He knew what needed to be done. What they'd been training for all this time. Plus, his country had little left except the legacy of the crates. The crates, whose technology could bring them back from poverty. Make them great again.

Like Japan.

He paced a little farther, vaguely aware that his behavior might disturb his men. He needed to walk this through in his mind, though. Assuming he could acquire the crates, as a worst-case scenario he was sure he knew someone who could find a buyer.

One word on the dark net would see to that.

He'd have to be careful, though. It wasn't his domain.

If not, maybe he could find someone sympathetic to their cause to help them leverage the technology. That would be the preferred option.

His hand slid to his pocket, searching for his pack of cigarettes.

Dammit. He'd already smoked them all.

He took a deep breath, trying to remember the calming effect their smoke had had on his lungs. It was all imagination now.

His men were carrying the last of the tent's pieces into the chopper as the engines fired up.

Ok, Benjiro, first things first. Take out the targets at the hangar and retrieve the crates.

He strode back toward the chopper while pulling up the screen to contact all the other operatives under his command. He was going to have to call in all the firepower he could put his hands on.

CHAPTER EIGHT

Japan, Mount Fuji in the distance

Where am I? Demon asked, perplexed. She could see the room and feel them moving through the room, but she couldn't feel her body.

I am taking you out of the room in a different type of…vehicle.

What is a vehicle?

What humans use to move around in, sometimes called a "car" or "truck" or "plane," Michael answered, realizing that he needed to get her to stop asking questions. He had never had a cat in his life, and he wasn't about to acquire one now.

Cats were always curious, and he was holding at least a semi-sentient cat due to Fuckwad up there playing with nanocytes. He sighed mentally. *What was he going to do with her?*

You know, she commented as Michael slipped through the door. The fire had caught and it was moving from the desk to a bookcase. Then the alarm sounded, and the fire sprinklers dropped from the ceiling and started spraying the room.

Sonofabitch! Michael grumped as he grabbed the three weres, who were still waiting for him at the bottom of the stairs where he had left them. Would wonders never cease?

He pulled the three of them into the Myst and was heading upstairs when the second-level door opened and two security guards headed down.

The two male Wechselbalg started cursing, so Michael snagged those two security guys and rounded up the third as he flew up to the next level.

"Who wants to play kill the security guards?" Michael asked, and wasn't too surprised to hear all three of the Wechselbalg volunteer.

The human security guys whimpered.

The three Level One security guards were heading toward the stairs when they got there, so he grabbed them as well.

One of them started screaming like a child seeing a monster movie.

Michael sped up as he went down a long hallway, ejecting that guard ten feet from the corner where his momentum slammed him into the concrete wall.

Michael stopped twenty feet later in a twenty-foot-square space, ejecting the three Wechselbalg first and giving them two seconds to prepare before he dropped the five remaining security guards one at a time, one second apart.

Once he had completed that effort, he headed toward the office in the corner.

He entered Raiden's office, where the man was ignoring the fire alarm to focus on his work.

Just as Michael had ordered.

HIM! Demon hissed in his mind. *He is the one who hurt me. He commanded those who captured me. Give him to me and I will work with you!*

Michael dropped Demon out of the Myst and solidified in the middle of the office. He would have informed the cat that he wasn't asking her to work with him.

But she was busy.

She had Raiden's neck in her mouth and had already bitten down. The blood sprayed his monitors as she pulled the struggling coder out of his seat.

Michael's eyebrows lifted as the man's gurgling screams finished just four seconds later.

Demon stood up and put her padded front feet on the desk as she growled her success. The fire in her eyes and the tail swishing behind her in exultation caused Michael to throw up his hands in defeat.

"Fuck it. Bethany Anne has a dog, and now I've got a cat." He smiled as he opened the door. "C'mon Demon, let's go see how the others are doing."

Michael? Akio called.

Yes?

The fire department has been called.

One second, Michael replied as he located the three Wechselbalg. Gaku had a clean hole through the muscle in his arm. "That will heal nicely," Michael told him.

Tanith was cleaning blood off her face. From the purple

bruises and what was left of a cut, one of the guards must have given her a good crack in the head.

Shiang was limping, and there was blood on his leg as well.

None of Raiden's guards were awake, however. "That one," Michael pointed to a guard who had apparently been thrown against the wall, "is still alive."

"What would you have us do?" Shiang asked. He wasn't asking belligerently, just wanted to know.

Michael pursed his lips and pulled a ball of Etheric energy into his hands. He casually tossed it onto the body, where it started melting the flesh. "Justice is served," Michael answered. As he started weaving a much larger ball of energy his writhing anger was barely constrained, and he focused on it until it was easily two feet across. "I will take you three away from this place," he told them. "I hope you don't need anything here?"

All three were just telling him they didn't when Michael pushed the ball away from him into a collection of cubicles. Flames immediately sprang forth. "Time to go!" Michael changed to Myst, grabbed the three Weres, Demon, and sped out of the room.

Michael grabbed the other programmer too and commanded her to sleep.

He would wipe her memory after they got out of the building.

Not finding any other heartbeats, he sent a command to Akio to stay back from the building. Six seconds later there was a massive explosion in the lower three levels, which destroyed them and caused the foundations to crack. Parts of the upper floors tilted and two windows shattered on the top level as furniture went through them to fall to the ground below.

Twenty minutes later the programmer walked back to her car in a daze. Michael, Demon, and Akio had left after speaking with the Wechselbalg.

They had a new lead on one of Raiden's partners.

By the time they reached the Pod, even Akio was straining under the weight of the cat's curiosity.

Abandoned Airfield, One Hundred Fifty Miles North-Northwest of Chengdu

The trees in the distance moved gently, the wind rustling in their limbs as the shadow solidified.

The black box touched down for the umpteenth time next the abandoned aircraft hangar. None of the military had been here in years, not since the fall of China. Shortly after WWDE things like their defense budget took a hit, along with most of their economy and people.

Mark was the first to hop out of the cabin, and he stretched as he looked around, taking in the scenery. He turned back to watch Jacqueline as he rubbed his arms. "You know, a hot shower and some hot chocolate would really be a treat right now." He jumped up and down to keep warm.

Jacqueline felt the cold and scooted back into the box for a blanket, which she wrapped around herself before going back outside.

"Thought Weres didn't feel the cold?" Sabine asked, trying to make conversation rather than antagonize her.

Jacqueline pulled a face. "I've gotten soft," she shot back

dryly. Mark started to snicker and then, realizing he was out of line, gave her a hug while the others disembarked.

Eve and Yuko pulled the last crate from the box, this time managing to carry it instead of dragging it. Sabine's senses searched their surroundings, peering into the darkness for any signs of movement.

Jacqueline noticed and wandered over to stand with her. "You think we're still being followed, don't you?"

Sabine shook her head slowly once, her attention only partially on Jacqueline. "I think it pays not to get complacent. And besides, my trigger finger is tingly."

Jacqueline frowned. "And that's a sign?"

She shrugged. "Could be."

Jacqueline gently exhaled through her nose in response and ambled into the hangar after the others.

Eve had been monitoring the place for several days before this day came—the day when the team finally united all the boxes that had been hidden by the Sacred Clan.

It wasn't much, but it was in a secure location and had electricity from a local generator. Power was still an issue in these parts, but it paid for the Chinese to still fund a precious few locations locally for clandestine operations, and for the sake of having servers and data centers in remote and almost untraceable areas.

The door closed automatically, leaving Sabine outside on her own. She started walking around the building, listening for any noise on the wind.

The heating clicked on inside in specific locations that Eve had earlier deemed to be most efficient.

No point in freezing their asses off before they got this mess assembled. And besides, the workspace needed to be fit for humans by the time Michael and Akio finally stopped killing people and got around to bringing them some geeks and engineers.

"So, uh, when do you think Michael might return?" Jacqueline asked Yuko and Eve as she followed them through the expanse of the place to the far end.

Eve cocked her head. "As soon as they're ready."

"And not a minute before," Yuko added playfully.

"Right," Jacqueline said. "But what about... I mean, we need to make sure we have food and stuff."

Yuko grinned at her. "Beautifully volunteered!" she exclaimed. The pair placed their heavy burden next to the other crates.

Yuko looked at the array, oblivious to Jacqueline's exclamation of protest at her latest assignment. "You know, I think we should start opening these in the morning. Get a start on it when we have proper light."

Eve glanced up at the old florescent lights, whose ballasts were barely able to function with most of the current being drawn by the heaters. "Probably a good idea," she agreed.

Mark had already started fondling the nearest crate. "You mean you're just going to let all this tech sit here unexamined for anyone to waltz in and steal out from under our noses? Without us getting to even touch it?"

Jacqueline growled. "No one is taking these from us. I've got this, Babe."

Mark grinned and winked. "You can be so romantic."

The whole hangar shuddered and all heads turned toward the door. Sabine was trying to close the enormous door behind her.

"Damn thing is so noisy," she grunted, tugging at it irritably.

Jacqueline visibly relaxed and called, "Nearly got your head taken off there, love."

Mark grinned. "Sounds like you're antsy, which means that you're hungry. How about we go find food for everyone and unwind?"

Yuko agreed and sent them on their way, with permission to use one of the Pods and take their time getting back.

Mark and Jacqueline, who still had a blanket wrapped around her, headed back across the hangar floor, passing Sabine on the way. Mark smiled, but Jacqueline mostly just nodded in her general direction.

Yup, she's angry all right, Mark thought, hurrying her along before anything else kicked off between the two women.

The Pod took off, barely visible beyond the perimeter of the airfield. All was calm...peaceful almost. A faint glow emanated from the hangar, again hardly visible.

Unless you knew what you were looking for.

Several hours later a black-ops stealth chopper flew into the vicinity, depositing a number of dark figures. The figures moved like shadows, but were armed to the hilt like the samurai of old—only with the most modern tech the Chinese government could afford.

They started hiking silently in the direction of the airfield.

CHAPTER NINE

Japan, Mount Fuji in the distance

Akio looked down at the mountain lion, who looked back up at him.

Food?

Michael smirked. "No, not food."

Akio's eyes narrowed. "Are you speaking to the cat?"

"Yes." Michael nodded at the three of them waited for transportation. He looked down. "Her name is Demon, and she was a science experiment for Raiden back there." Michael jerked his head in the direction of the orange glow reflecting from the clouds and smoke in the night sky. "Apparently he was doing research into programming things with nanocytes, and injected her with enough of them that the nanocytes have been trying to help her."

Akio bowed slightly to the cat. "Welcome, Demon. I am Akio." He waved a finger. "And I am not food."

Demon sniffed and looked around. *I wasn't asking if you were food.*

Akio could just detect the mental connection. It was

solid, if faint, and she seemed to have a dry sense of humor. *I was asking if there* was *food.*

"Oh? I seemed to have misunderstood."

Michael looked around, a smile playing at the very corners of his mouth.

Akio glanced at Michael, his eyebrows pulling together in thought. "There is a park approximately three miles in that direction." He pointed north. "There should be something there."

Michael's head swiveled in that direction. "We will head there to see if she can find anything." As Akio nodded his understanding, Michael and Demon disappeared.

Akio looked around in the night, his hands behind his back. He had considered sending them five miles to the west.

There was an amusement park in that direction.

He could always explain that he had gotten his parks confused.

Michael stood under a large tree next to a moonlit clearing fifty yards in diameter as the X-wing Pod silently lowered itself in the darkness.

Akio jumped out of the ship and made his way over to him. "She is almost done," Michael answered the unasked question. "It seems she doesn't like to be watched as she eats fresh kills."

Akio turned his head in the direction of the sound of the crunching of small bones in the massive jaws of the cat. "Am I to assume you have adopted a cat?"

Michael shrugged. "Bethany Anne has Ashur, or at least I assume she still does?" He glanced at Akio, who shrugged in his ignorance. "Well, she had Ashur in the past, so I don't think it will be a problem."

"You know that cats do not have masters, unlike dogs, correct?" Akio asked. "They have slaves. Or if you are lucky, they have housemates who fetch them water and open their food containers. They go to the store, clean out the kitty litter—"

Akio stopped speaking for a moment, then snorted. "That's going to be a very large litter box."

Michael opened his mouth to argue, then shut it. "We will adapt, I'm sure." The two of them could hear rustling as Demon finished her meal. "Plus, I will explain outer space and what it means to have to walk back." Michael smirked. "She is smart enough to understand."

<hr>

Demon walked through the park, enjoying the sensation of the grass on the pads of her feet. A slight feeling of sadness swept through her as she considered her paws, which had no claws.

They had been removed.

Even finding and killing this whatever-she-had-just-eaten had been a challenge. One of the chases had found her turning quickly, only to have her legs slide out from underneath her. She had rolled over and over before hitting a tree.

While capturing her own food had been nice, acknowl-edging the loss of a part of her was difficult.

She could hear Michael speak to the non-food, Akio. So he had arrived. Demon smiled, and shrank, willing herself to become as small as possible as she slunk through the undergrowth, her tail twitching.

Both men looked at the tablet. "Eve connected us with the police," he updated Michael. "The one we seek has a team of fighters who killed some high-level political figures right after Yuko had tied them up. They will need to be notified of any takedown we accomplish so they can close the case."

Michael glanced at the map. "This is the middle of downtown?" When Akio nodded, Michael asked, "Does it not seem odd that such a Clan would have their base in the middle of town?"

"Not really, no," Akio answered. "This group fights well, but they probably sell their services. It is easier to hide in the middle of the city than to have us track them to a remote location using vehicles."

Michael nodded his understanding.

Akio glanced at the time. "We can do this tonight, or we can wait."

Michael leaned back to peer at Akio from a distance. "Wait?" He smiled. "What is this 'wait' you speak of?"

Demon had made it to some bushes just two pounces away from the men. Michael had his back to her, and Akio could not see through the man.

It was perfect.

Akio was about to answer Michael's question regarding the meaning of "wait" when Michael blazed into action. He twisted and ducked as a figure leapt over him, headed straight for Akio.

Akio set his legs, his right arm reaching up and under the head of the cat as his left braced to catch the rib cage.

The cat slammed into him, making a gurgling sound as Akio whipped Demon against the Black Eagle.

Ouuuuuch! Demon keened as Akio dropped her. *My heeeeaaaad!*

"And *that* is why Akio is not food," Michael told the mountain lion as she wove in a crooked line while trying to catch a breath.

You did that on purpose? Akio asked in surprise.

I've been working to cover her noise, Michael admitted. *She has to learn she isn't the apex predator anymore.*

The big cat laid on the ground after Akio released her. *That was painful.*

"You should not have tried to sneak up on us," Michael reprimanded her. "You could have been killed."

She sighed. *I was playing! Who knew Akio was so fast?* She turned her head to look at Akio, who was staring at her with one eyebrow raised. *And what happened with your eyes?*

Akio didn't answer. He merely glanced to Michael, who answered, "They flashed red."

Oh.

Akio pointed to himself. "I am a vampire, as is Michael. Occasionally, when we are angry or surprised, our connection to the Etheric will cause our eyes to flash red as you saw."

Like the others flashed the color of the daytime?

"Yellow," Michael told her. "Akio's were red."

I caught red the first time. She licked a paw. *It's not like I'm a dog, here. My lack of claws doesn't make me stupid.*

Akio glanced at Michael.

Michael sighed.

Getting her acclimated to Ashur might prove to be a challenge.

"Let's look at your paws, Demon," Michael told her as he walked over to where she was laying down. "And if you so much as look at me wrong, I will backhand you so hard you will roll until you hit the sea."

She looked up at him. *What's the sea?*

"Large body of salt water," Michael replied.

What's salt water? she followed up.

"Water with salt in it," Michael answered, turning her paw over in his hand.

How far away is that, and in what direction? she asked, trying to twist her head to look around.

Michael's shoulders slumped and Akio turned around, not allowing Michael to see him cover his mouth or the glint of laughter in his eyes.

<u>Downtown Tokyo, Japan</u>

The black Pod slipped through the upper atmosphere toward the massive city of lights. "They have full holographic advertisements?" Michael asked. He didn't bother to hide his shock as he watched enormous holograms a hundred feet high—or higher, in two cases—spread their marketing messages in the night.

There was no need for the sun. The sheer amount of light in the city was enough to permit them to walk around.

Shadows, he surmised, might be hard to find on the major streets below the massive skyscrapers. Everywhere he looked, he saw floating and flying vehicles.

The two had dropped Demon off at one of Akio's safehouses just south of the city. Michael had promised that eventually he would get her claws back for her, and Akio had just happened to have his tablet in a position to take a photo of Demon licking Michael's face in appreciation. He had grimaced as the cat's tongue scraped the side of his cheek.

It was good blackmail material for the future.

"Yes, there were some movies back before WWDE which imagined the reality of what Japan is now."

"Very impressive," Michael commented as Akio took them around the largest area of lights and ads and dropped them onto a medium-height seventy-five story building that was in the shade of a larger two-hundred-story building. "Just pop the hatch. I'll take us down," Michael told him.

A moment later the black Pod shot into the air to hide amongst the clouds as two men appeared on the roof of the tall building. Looking over the side, Michael pointed. "Is it that one?" he asked. Akio followed his finger.

Pulling up his tablet, Akio used the zoom feature. "That building with the blue lights?" Akio asked.

"Yes."

"No." Akio shook his head. "It is the older-looking building to the side."

"Of course it is." Michael nodded once and the two of them disappeared into his Myst.

Orochi nodded as Aoi walked by him. He was standing in the sacred area inside their true base of operations.

The building next to them was a plant. While he had excellent contacts inside the police force, you never trusted any party whose purpose put them at odds with your own. At some point you would be enemies.

It was just a given.

He had tried to get hold of Raiden twice before his contact alerted him to a very suspect fire at one of Raiden's businesses. Orochi sighed.

Raiden wasn't the only one who had the ability to uncover secrets. He had probably gone to ground at that building at the instigation of his partner. Unfortunately, it seemed that the Diplomat—or others—was smarter.

Which left him with his own challenge. Should he withdraw his people, or just himself?

Cut off the root, the vine would die. Cut off the vine, the root can grow again. He nodded sharply to himself.

As the root, he needed to stay safe. Decision made, he stepped toward his office. He was walking down the underground hallway when the lights dimmed and the red safety lights turned on.

Something had tripped his security next door.

His lips pressed together as he reached his office. He grabbed his wakizashi, the shorter of his swords, which was designed for inside work, and also pocketed a few extra tricks as he readied himself in case the attackers were to successfully repulse his first response and figure out how to make it into this enclave.

There was no running from a fight. While not the most tactically sound business choice, there was no way he would fail his teams by running like a coward.

He held his sword by the sheath and walked toward the security room to watch what happened next.

"Yessss." Michael stood in the middle of a large practice area, slowly rotating to scan for enemies as Akio, only five feet away, watched the hallways. "I do believe we have kicked over an anthill." Reaching under his jacket, Michael pulled out a short sword. "This might be a little fun."

Do you have a connection to the leader?

There was a lag before Michael answered, *Got him. He isn't going to run from the fight. Interesting, they aren't in this building.*

Hai! Akio looked around. As far as he could tell they would come through the four entrances into the large room. However, he'd rather be safe than either dead or painfully mending while Michael laughed at him with a big fat, "I told you so."

Not that he expected Michael to say that, in so many words.

"Eve is going to be pissed she got the address wrong," Akio whispered. "She prides herself on accuracy."

"Pride comes before the fall," Michael answered. "I should know, I coined the phrase." He chuckled. "It wasn't about me originally, even though I just proved it." He finished as they heard the rushing footsteps whispering through the hallways and they got themselves into position.

Akio limbered up. "I count eighty-eight." He sighed. "Somebody must have been expecting us."

"Probably a reaction to Raiden's death," Michael answered as the entrances vomited fighters. Soon they had four groups of just over twenty men each. "I'll take the first fifty. You can have the rest."

Akio grunted. "I'll leave you twenty, because I am respectful," he told him with a genuine smile on his face.

Akio chuckled as Michael spoke to those around them. "You sexist bastards! I know you have women in your party. Why aren't you letting them play too? Scared they will prove they are the better sex?"

Michael received no verbal response, but a few of the men focused on him. "That is not playing with honor!" Akio told him. "You are sucking them toward you."

"The only rule in this game is that you must use only sword or fists unless they use guns," Michael told him.

"*Hai!*" Akio agreed, "And no using Etheric magic."

Michael sniffed. "I don't do *magic*." He headed toward the nearest group of fighters as Akio went in the other direction.

CHAPTER TEN

Haru's eyes narrowed when the man in the black hat asked about the women. Truthfully, they did have women in their ranks, but they were rather rare. Two were not good enough to join them for this fight, and two were not at the base at the moment. The last was superior to all of them, and was guarding Orochi-sama.

Still, he hoped his was the sword which would pierce this arrogant *gaijin* ass.

His group opened up to allow them plenty of room to swing their swords, but not so far apart that they couldn't protect one another.

Then the two men attacked.

The Japanese warrior went to the far side of the dojo and the *gaijin* came to his group.

Perfect!

That was, until the dying started.

Haru led off, circling to his left. The man in black was in the middle of his brothers and there was nothing but screaming, both as various men attacked and in pain as hands were cut off, throats sliced, and bodies violently kicked upward to hit walls two body-heights above them.

This man was not human.

Pressing his lips together, he ran toward the attacker in a crouch and struck upward with his sword. He gaped in shock as his sword sliced through the space where the man had been. He looked behind him, and while the attacker wasn't exactly in the same spot, Haru's sword should have hit him.

A voice spoke in his mind. *Nice try! You can come again if you want a second pass.*

A vampire. Haru gripped his sword tightly, already running back toward the creature. Knowledge known is knowledge used. And knowledge was—

The wakizashi erupted from the back of Haru's head as Michael jumped over the slash the now-dead fighter had launched at him. As he yanked it out Haru's body dropped to the floor, and Michael's macabre dance of death continued.

"Sixteen!" he yelled.

Akio chose to wade into the mass of fighters. He blocked the first two slashes that came at him and flicked his sword to the right, slicing a neck open as his left hand batted a sword to the side. He grabbed that fighter's clothes and pulled, sliding the surprised man around to place him right where the two others on his right were attacking.

He let go of his pincushion, the two fighters saying nothing as their teammate dropped to the floor.

He noted that Michael had already put five on the ground and, setting his lips, he upped his speed. He batted two swords aside and his horizontal slice took two more heads as he kicked behind him, driving back several who were trying to flank him.

Glancing over his shoulder, he saw that none of those who had been knocked off-balance by his kick had hurt each other.

Pity, that.

He was up to four and moved his body slightly to the left, the sword that had been aimed at him harmlessly stabbing air where his chest had been a moment before.

A sharp slice downward and the arm bearing the sword was severed, the sword now falling with the hand still attached. A second later Akio cut his head off. Those who lost limbs rarely maintained situational awareness.

Five.

He twisted to his right and stabbed, pulling the fighter he impaled toward him and grabbing his sword with his other hand. "I have need of this," Akio told him as he yanked his sword back out of the fighter's chest. "And you don't."

Six.

Now his dance of death was vastly improved.

Two slices, and he was up to eight. A block, a parry, and two more cuts made it ten.

Michael's voice reverberated off the walls. "Sixteen!"

Akio's lips pressed together and those around him who could see his eyes hesitated for a moment.

Which was enough for Akio to quickly take down four more.

Michael glanced at Akio as he blocked two thrusts on landing from a rather theatrical jump.

He had just downed four guards in the space of an eyeblink.

Dammit, he shouldn't have been playing around. He turned toward the nearest fighter, his eyes flashing red. "I'll be taking that!" He blocked the first thrust, then grabbed the hand with the sword and cut it off, backhanding the fighter in the face. As the man screamed blood sprayed from his arm, causing the two at his side to wipe their eyes.

Michael dispatched them both quickly as he worked to get the hand unclenched from the sword. Now bearing two swords, he upped his speed once more.

He and Akio worked counterclockwise, running through the fighters like a pair of mobile Cuisinart blenders.

"Eighteen," Akio shouted.

"Twenty-one!" Michael replied.

Back and forth the two went, not offering or asking or giving quarter as the battle raged. Swords clashed blade-on-blade as one group tried desperately to kill the two, but the results were obvious and soon enough the truth became reality when the last kill slid off the end of Akio's sword.

He turned to Michael. "Forty-one."

Michael was leaning against the wall. "I was waiting for you to catch up," he told him. Pushing off the wall, he pointed toward the corridor. "We have more that way."

Akio cleaned his personal blade on a nearby body.

"After you," he replied as he followed Michael into the northernmost hallway.

Thirty seconds later the two of them faced an old brick wall.

Michael was frowning as he listened to the thoughts of those in the building on the other side. "Guns! They are bringing guns to a swordfight."

"*Hai.*" Akio sighed. "I am ashamed of their actions," he said as he sheathed his sword and tossed the other away. Reaching back, he grabbed a pistol and pulled it out. "On the other hand, it will be less sticky this way."

"True," Michael agreed. He had already sheathed his sword and pulled his Jean Dukes. "Swords can be rather messy." He and Akio looked at each other, both of them smiling. "Ready?"

Akio nodded. "*Hai!*"

Michael disappeared first, with Akio disappearing in his Myst a blink of an eye later.

Abandoned Airfield, One Hundred Fifty Miles North-Northwest of Chengdu

"Well, hell," Eve said, using a bit of her brainpower to continue her effort toward sounding human. "It seems that you were right," she finished, pointing to a screen on her tablet. "The Pod's systems have detected tangos inbound from the northeast."

Yuko bit her lip, thinking of her options as she considered the force coming for them. "They won't want to bomb us and risk destroying the technology."

"Mark and Jacqueline?" Eve asked as Sabine walked over to listen to the conversation.

"Leave them out of this," said Yuko, her tone crystalizing her decision. "Get me a connection to Akio."

"Ohhh." Eve touched the screen.

"This is Akio," his deep voice answered. The three of them heard an explosion in the background, followed by a scream, then silence. "I am sorry about that."

Yuko ignored the noise. "Is this an appropriate time to talk?"

"Certainly," he replied. "Michael, would you be so kind as to take out those three over there? I need a moment with Yuko." There was more screaming in the background, then the battle sounds faded a bit.

Yuko leaned forward. "Is Michael going to be OK?"

Akio chuckled. "These are not the best fighters. They use guns."

"That is what makes them not the best fighters?" Sabine asked from the background. When Eve and Yuko turned to look at her, she blushed and mouthed "Sorry."

Akio ignored the byplay. "I believe we have about five more to dispatch." There was a slight pause. "Four more. So how can we help you?"

Yuko spoke up. "There are at least two hundred coming here to attack the base. Mark and Jacqueline are not here, just me, Eve, and Sabine. I'm wondering if you have the time to join us so we don't have to patch holes in the building."

"Who is it?" Akio asked.

"Chinese," Eve responded. "I've finally found their working frequency."

"Michael has two left, so we can be out of this building in sixty seconds. Make sure you tell the police to come clean up," he continued. "I've seen plenty of evidence these are the ones who killed the Emperor, so there shouldn't be a backlash about leaving no one alive."

"I guess it's too late to save one?" Eve asked, sending a message to the police contact on behalf of Yuko.

"It's Michael," Akio replied, as if that answered everything.

Eve sent additional messages "The Pod will be there in thirty seconds. It will deposit you in the west to allow you to come up behind them." She looked at Yuko, who put up seven fingers. "You will have seven minutes to kill them before we have to mount a defense."

There was a short pause before Akio answered, "Understood. Akio out." He cut the connection.

A significant distance away, two men started arguing about body counts as they moved to the roof.

If anyone had been left in the building they would have heard one man respond, "No, you told me to go ahead—that you had a call—so those kills count. I'll forgive you two, but not the others…"

Their discussion muted as they went through the door to the roof. In the distance, police sirens could be heard heading toward that area of town.

Abandoned Airfield, One Hundred Fifty Miles North-Northwest of Chengdu

The two hundred men moved silently through the

underbrush, taking their time and checking their devices to see if they had been caught.

So far no one seemed to be doing anything odd inside the building. There were no strange noises or lights.

They had maybe ten minutes to go before they would be in place to charge the building, using their advantage of surprise to overcome those inside. Until they had eyes on the target they couldn't fire their weapons.

If anything was damaged someone in the team would be blamed, and at best demoted. At worst, if the damage was caused by negligence, court-martialed.

And then stuck in prison or killed. It depended on one's connections.

Chang grimaced as he thought about this. There were a couple in his platoon who would get off scot-free if they were the offending parties.

It was good to have family in high places.

He glanced at his screen and then had to glance again.

His team had lost five connections since the last time he had looked. He paused, holding his fist in the air to halt those around him as he worked to understand the problem, and his command rippled out silently until everyone had stopped moving.

His eyebrows narrowed in thought, then his eyes widened in concern. He didn't bother to be quiet this time. "Turn around!" he called. "Ambush!"

He did as he told them to do, turning and lifting his rifle to his shoulder. Many around him did the same. "Support!" he commanded as they went back the way they had come.

The second time he had looked his platoon had dropped by another fifteen connections.

His team was being decimated.

Yuko put her feet up as she sat in a chair sipping tea.

Sabine looked at her from her chair a few feet away. "You aren't worried?"

"No," Yuko admitted, taking another small sip. "They have started their attack. No one will get through," she said, nodding toward the door.

"There were a lot of dots on the screen," Sabine pressed. "You don't think I should go out and make sure none get this far?"

Yuko shook her head. "Oh, definitely not. That would be a waste of your time."

"She is right," Eve admitted, turning away from her computer screen. She lifted a tablet and touched it twice before handing it to Sabine. "Feel free to watch the dots disappear if you would like. Already they are down over thirty percent."

Sabine watched the dots steadily decrease, and suddenly those that were closest to the hangar moved away.

Heading to their deaths.

Yuko continued sipping her tea, the occasional scream and or rifle shot piercing her thoughts. "Eve?" When she looked up, her friend was staring at her. "We are going to have to do something about the Chinese government. They have—" She turned her head to the side as the door started squeaking open.

"One hundred ten," Akio said definitively. "If you allow for the two back in Tokyo, Michael-san, we are even."

Michael closed the door as if it weighed nothing. "We are even, then. I will grant you those two easily." The two men turned to see the three ladies staring at them. They looked down, taking note of all the leaves, grass, blood, and gore on their bodies. Yuko was holding a cup of tea in one hand and a plate in the other. She nodded to her right and smiled. "The showers, gentlemen, are that way."

Both men stood a bit straighter and headed off to the ladies' right, mischievous smiles on their face.

"Do you think they have been up to something?" Sabine asked, watching the two men head into a hallway,

"I've no idea, but with men it's always safer to assume they were," Yuko admitted.

Michael and Akio came out about ten minutes later. Michael didn't have his coat or his shirt on, just some pants he had found in the back. Akio came out in a robe.

"Because," Michael said, finishing a comment he had been making to Akio, "the robes are made for shorter humans. I refuse to wear a robe that looks like a child's jacket."

"I prefer the term 'properly sized,'" Akio replied, his clipped Japanese accent precise.

"You mean to say I am brutishly large?" Michael asked, slipping into a proper English accent.

Eve put up an arm to get Michael and Akio's attention. As they focused on her, this movement also caused Yuko's and Sabine's attention to return to her as well.

Although Sabine took one more look at Michael as she turned.

"Oh, *this* should be interesting," Eve said, as a request to communicate arrived from the Chinese military.

<u>Abandoned Airfield, One Hundred Fifty Miles North-Northwest of Chengdu</u>

"You don't wish to put any more clothes on?" Yuko asked, pointedly looking at Michael's chest, then abs, then chest again before returning her gaze to his eyes, raising her eyebrows in inquiry.

Michael looked down and then back at her as he smiled. "I don't intend to be on camera, Diplomat. That is your role, is it not?" She rolled her eyes and walked over to stand in front of the camera.

Eve moved out of the way of the video stream before she hit the **ACCEPT** button.

A Chinese official was smoothing his jacket when he realized he was live.

He glanced off-camera, annoyed, before turning his attention to the screen in front of him with a smile now pasted on his face. "Hello, Diplomat. My name is Longwei." He shook his head, exasperated. "Why am I not surprised?"

Yuko, her face impassive, simply shrugged. "Surprised at what?"

"That you have dishonored our sovereignty and attacked our people."

"You mean we defended ourselves from your attack, perhaps?" Yuko replied. "I can assure you I never got out of my chair. If something happened, it was not me."

The man on the screen tried to compose himself, suppressing his flash of anger. "I have received assurance from our contacts in Japan that the killers of our Emperor have been found. Unfortunately, I am told the whole group were killed in horrendous ways. Our contacts in the police department suggested that the deaths were not normal."

Yuko smiled. "I am so happy to hear you have found the killers. I did express through channels that I and my team had nothing to do with these deaths."

"Perhaps," he replied. "Perhaps not. Either way, because of this I offer you and those with you the chance to walk out of our sovereign land, taking only that which is on your back and leaving all else…" The man kept talking; his lips were moving, but no one in the hangar heard a word.

Yuko frowned and turned toward Eve. "Why can't I hear him?" Eve was busy on the computer's keyboard.

Longwei's eyes narrowed when the Diplomat seemingly ignored him, turning to the side. She was talking, but he couldn't hear her.

The technician to his right side was busy at his controls. "She can't hear us, sir!" he said, and flushed in embarrassment before turning to Longwei. "We are blocked from speech, sir."

A second later the video went black and Longwei could hear the Diplomat again. "What do you mean, 'It is neither of us?'"

Another voice replied to the Diplomat, "I have run the diagnostics. This is outside interference." There was a pause. "Ok, they have changed the interference. We can hear them now, but not see their video."

Longwei chewed his lip. Should he continue as if this were their problem, or admit he knew they weren't responsible?

The Diplomat continued, "Honorable Longwei, as you can tell we have been interrupted. While I can't see you, or you me, I believe we can proceed with our conversation. You, sir, were in the middle of demanding we leave. I will permit you thirty seconds to continue your tirade before I reply."

"There can be no rebuttal!" Longwei ground out. He preferred to see those he intended to cow. While the Diplomat was considered a dragon you could not contain, it was his job to secure the artifacts he had been told would be at this location.

"Longwei, we both know you wish to have something in my possession. I know, even if you don't, that this won't happen. I have the appropriate—"

Her voice was cut off as a new face appeared on the screen—a Caucasian face, and American, if Longwei had to guess. He tried to speak to the Diplomat, but his technician simply shook his head.

"This is a one-way communication, sir," he told

Longwei.

All the screens in the command center now displayed the face on his screen and Longwei's eyes narrowed. She reminded him of someone, but he couldn't place where he had seen her before.

"Hello," she started, her eyes staring through the screen as if she were peering into his soul and his brain. "I am Bethany Anne Nacht. My ships will be arriving in approximately four days. Your telescopes will start to see the evidence of our armada shortly. I am providing this video on known government frequencies to allow you a chance to minimize the frenzy a space fleet might cause over Earth. You have been notified. If you happen to have my love in anything less than the best shape, I will rip your country apart and bury you under it."

She smiled happily. "Otherwise, have a good day!"

The video blanked, leaving Longwei staring at the Diplomat again. She seemed to be staring through him.

Longwei got his voice back. "Who was that?"

The Diplomat refocused on Longwei, answering his question honestly if in a subdued voice. "That was my Queen," she replied, reaching up to wipe a tear from her eye. "And my friend," she finished. Looking down, oblivious to Longwei, she whispered loudly enough for him to hear her. "She came *back*."

Longwei asked, his bluster gone, "What does she mean, 'ships and armada?'"

A female voice answered from off-screen. "Sending you the data now," he was told.

The technician who was working with him whipped around and whispered to the two men to his right, and soon all three of their screens changed to different pictures.

On the screens were pictures of a large circle in space behind spaceships…

Dozens and dozens of spaceships, with one image showing a massive ship. Who knew how large it was, since there was nothing on the screen to compare it with?

"Oh, spaceships," was all he said. A moment later his eyes narrowed.

"Warships."

He turned back to the screen. "Who is this 'love' of hers? We do not have any space people captive that I know of."

The Diplomat turned to her right, then stepped out of the way and left the camera's range. A huge man took her place, his perfect six-pack showing on the screen. "Do you think," he asked someone off-camera, his American accent precise, "I could maybe…I don't know, *not* show my stomach to him?"

There were some snickers before someone adjusted the video up. Longwei saw a man with dark hair and a… cowboy hat?…on his head. He smiled at Longwei. "That would be me." His eyes flashed red and his fangs extended. "Feel free to try to come get me, if you wish."

Longwei, sweat pooling at the top of his forehead, started vigorously shaking his head. "No. Please," he put a hand up, "stay safely right where you are, and we will make sure nothing happens to you or your people."

Soon after that the connection was broken.

Sabine stood up and stretched. "Well, that was exciting!"

She smiled as the image of Bethany Anne came back up on the screen.

Michael was staring at her.

"So," Sabine asked, coming up beside Michael, "what's it feel like to have your girlfriend save you?"

Michael chuckled. "It wasn't the first time," he replied, and turned around. "I've got to see if my clothes are clean."

Two minutes after Michael disappeared to check on his clothes, the hangar door opened and Mark and Jacqueline stepped in. "Why do I smell a lot of blood?" Jacqueline asked, her face scrunched. "It's nasty."

She spotted Akio. "Oh, you two are back?" She put a hand to her mouth, "Oh my God, I'm so sorry for saying you smell!" As the two walked closer, her eyes narrowed. "Wait a minute, you're clean!" She looked around the hangar. "Where's Michael?"

Her curiosity was put on hold when Mark asked, "Who's *she?*"

Jacqueline whipped around, eyes narrowing at a picture of an image of a woman with black hair, her eyes full of anger so deep even Jacqueline was cowed.

"That," Yuko whispered, "is Bethany *Anne*."

One Hundred Hours Later, Japan

All over Japan video screens changed, showing the same announcement in unison.

"Hello." Her voice was the same as that which had been recorded by multiple governments recently, and which many had found in their historical archives.

She was the living embodiment of history.

"My name is Bethany Anne Nacht, and I was at one time the leader of TQB Enterprises. I have come back to Earth to set up a planetary orbital defense system. We call it the 'BYPS system.'"

"I am going to arrive over your country in twenty-four hours. Well, I and some of my ships. We are going to meet with our people who are in your country, and then around the world. We are not here to attack you, so do not attack us." Her eyes flared red. "If we are attacked, be aware I *will* rain fire and destruction on those who attack us, the likes of which have not been seen in the history of our planet."

Her lips pressed together. "While I care about your safety, do not expect my concern to supersede my responsibility to my people. If you attack, you will be destroyed."

She leaned back in her chair and smiled. "Michael, I am back."

The video blacked out.

The video went around the world, shooting from house to house of those who had the ability to receive the information faster than the previously utilized notification mechanism...

Gossip.

Most started wondering, who was this goddess—the Queen Bitch—and who was her counterpart, Michael? Was she the new mother of Earth, and he the father?

Humans have a proclivity to follow deities. If they do not believe in the Christian God, they will occasionally worship rocks.

Or plants, birds, wolves, bears, their elders... The list goes on and on.

At that moment many started a *new* religion. Their

deity's eyes flared red when she was angry. She had tried to protect the Earth, but those on Earth had killed each other. Now she was back to offer protection.

Perhaps this time she would do something for her people, or was the Matriarch too displeased with humanity to care?

Only time would tell.

Michael and his group got into the ships, which lifted silently into the air. Eve had contacted ADAM, who was sending protection to watch over the hangar.

While Eve was pretty sure the Chinese government was not going to attack the area, she couldn't be sure the news hadn't made it out to those who sought the relics for themselves.

As the Pods left, a lone ship sliced down through the heavens and the clouds flared red as it banked hard, the captain of the ship shouting his joy. Human eyes peered into the sky as the spaceship passed overhead.

Soon it was slowing down, circling three miles out from their designated operations area. They were here to protect something for the Queen Bitch.

The *G'laxix Sphaea* slowed to a crawl. Fifty feet above the asphalt outside the warehouse, the back hatch opened. Had anyone been there, they would have seen twelve bodies in armored suits, some larger than others, jump down to land on the broken-up concrete.

"How are you doing?" the captain of the ship called

down to his military leader from his position in the rear hatch.

Kiel punched a button on the side of his head and his visor and shield retracted. He pulled in a huge amount of air to fill his lungs and blew it back out before answering his captain.

"Feels good to be back, Kael-ven. It feels good to be back." Then the military commander put his visor back down marked eleven locations on his HUD, and sent his team into the area around the warehouse.

To make damned sure no one touched the Queen's property.

CHAPTER TWELVE

<u>Safehouse outside Tokyo, Japan</u>

"Are you kidding me?" Yuko had her hands on her hips and was staring up at Michael, who had just come out of his room.

"What?" He looked down at himself and then at her again, a puzzled look on his face.

"You aren't going to wear *that* outfit, are you?" Yuko asked. She had some clothes in her hands, and she grimaced and draped them over the nearest chair. "Never mind. You should save these until after the reunion."

Michael smiled, but as Yuko turned back to him his smile changed to a look of concentration. "Why? Are you thinking the reunion might cause a problem with the health of the clothes?"

Yuko walked up to Michael and patted him on the chest between the lapels of his open coat. She shook her head. "I love you, Michael, but sometimes you are such a *man*." She patted him one more time before stepping around him to exit the room. "At least you showered!" she called back. "We are leaving in five minutes, everyone!"

"So…" Sabine walked by and took a look at Michael before nodding sharply. "Good choice." She glanced at the nicer clothes over the chair. "Wise man. Wise man indeed," she said as continued. "I've got to grab something out of the Pod, be right back!"

Michael watched Sabine head out of the room and then out the front door. Mark and Jacqueline came through the hallway a moment later. "Hi!" the Were said excitedly. Michael wasn't sure if she had seen the other set of clothes or not when she stopped, put her hand to her lips, and looked him up and down. "I suppose for the first time together, that might actually be the best choice." She shrugged. "But I'm just guessing, based on what I've heard."

"Why?" Michael asked, his eyes narrowing. "What have you heard?"

Mark reacted to the elbow to his ribs and started walking toward the door as Jacqueline waved. "Sorry, Dad, but Yuko said we have to go. Time's a-wasting!"

"Where's Eve?" Michael asked the room.

Akio answered as he buttoned up his shirt. "Mmmmm." He looked Michael over. "Interesting. And Eve," he said, snagging Michael's arm, "is outside already. As you should be if you don't want to miss the entrance of your mate."

A moment later the front door clicked as it closed, and Demon walked into the room, laid down, and closed her eyes.

Should anyone come in except Michael's people, there would be hell to pay.

A few minutes later, Sabine entered through the front

door and walked to the couch. "We got guard duty," She told Demon as she picked up a magazine. A moment later, she looked over to the cat, "Think we will get lucky and someone will try to attack us?"

<u>Tokyo, Japan</u>

The city had suspended work and school, and everyone who could had gone outside.

They were coming.

Their anxiety was laced with excitement. Those who were excited held the shoulders of those who wanted to believe but feared everything new.

Especially when the 'new' were massive spaceships coming from unknown parts of the galaxy.

The pundits on television were showing clips from an archived movie called *Independence Day* and explaining that the ships would be arriving through the atmosphere with the fire roiling off their outer skins. Due to the incredible amount of heat their ships would be radiating, there would be massive flaming balls coming down through the atmosphere to land—or rather crash—and kill anyone too close.

The reality, as it turned out, was similar, yet completely different.

There were many clouds the day the Queen returned, and her ships gracefully pierced the planet's atmosphere, descending over the course of thousands of miles as they headed across the Pacific Ocean toward the islands of Japan.

Those on the ground who were looking to the east

started pointing when the clouds were pushed out of the way as if something massive was parting them.

Then a ship broke through the curtain of white, and the people on the ground collectively drew in their breaths. A few called to those around them to look at what they were already seeing.

Then more started pointing—something else was in the clouds. Moments later two more ships broke through, and now there were three ships majestically slicing through the air.

On the south side of Yoyogi Park, six individuals strode through the entrance and walked toward a large open area.

Two were obviously of Japanese heritage, and two were younger Americans. The fifth was a smaller being, either an older child or a short adult.

And there was also a man in an overcoat, with a cowboy hat covering his short hair.

No one paid attention to the weapons they had stashed about their bodies. Japan was very aware of those who could change into creatures, and while the citizens had not supported weapons before WWDE (World's Worst Day Ever), they'd had to learn to live with the risk of shooting one another when their only other choice was being gutted by werewolves.

It wasn't in the DNA of the Japanese to lie down and accept defeat without a fight, so after WWDE when the werewolves made themselves known, the Japanese took a hard look at their laws, and weapons were back on the table.

One had better know how to use them, however.

The six who walked through Yoyogi Park wore their weapons as an extension of themselves.

Especially the two older men.

Michael gazed at the three massive spaceships headed in his direction, then turned to Akio and nodded to the sky. "She sure knows how to make an entrance, doesn't she?"

"*Hai!*" Akio agreed, a small smile playing on his lips.

His Queen had come back, and he had retained his Honor and brought her loved one back to her—no matter how many times Michael had tried to get himself killed in the process.

Which had been a lot.

QBS *ArchAngel II*, Bethany Anne's Suite

"Hell, no!" Bethany Anne told Gabrielle, who was pointing to the armor in the closet. "I'll not be stuck wearing a full set of armor!" She jerked her thumb toward the ground. "I'm going down, and I'm going down now. I can feel him!"

"At *least* put on your chest armor!" Gabrielle argued, holding out the two pieces. "Let's not get shot in the chest, shall we?" she asked Bethany Anne, who stopped and looked at what Gabrielle was offering her.

Bethany Anne blurred, and Gabrielle found that the armor she'd held a moment earlier was now missing.

"Bethany Anne?" She looked around and stepped into the armor closet. "BA?" Her muffled voice was audible outside of the bedroom. A moment later, she came out to find John and Eric suited up and waiting for the two of them.

Gabrielle flicked her hand. "Let's go. She's already split."

John smiled at Eric, who shook his head. "I know, I know," Eric said as the three of them left the suite and started toward the ship's bays. "You won!"

Yoyogi Park, Tokyo, Japan

There were two distinct scenarios available to those who had chosen Yoyogi Park from which to view the arrival of the Queen.

One group watched as a smaller craft flew out of the capital ship in the middle of the formation and headed toward the park.

The other group was near the six in the clearing when a woman and a white dog suddenly appeared ten feet above the ground, then fell to the earth. She looked around for one second before spotting the man she was searching for.

She had on boots, black leather pants, and a black blouse over a skintight shirt of some alien substance, and she wore a gold necklace. She and the dog started walking toward the six. The man in the cowboy hat strode ahead of the others, his eyes for her alone.

That their bodies crashed together hinted at the speed at which they had been moving, and their subsequent torrid kiss proved these two knew each other.

Very well indeed.

The other five stopped some ten paces back.

The two separated, and her eyes flashed as her hand streaked upward to slap the man.

Who caught her wrist.

"Let go of me!" Bethany Anne snarled, then hissed, "You owe me for dying!"

"I think not." Michael shook his head. "Let's not discuss these last one hundred and fifty-plus years. My Honor demanded I come back, and here I am."

"I didn't say," she growled, "that you should take so fucking *LONG!*" She ripped her arm out of his grip and poked him in the chest with a finger. "Do you know how much shit I've had to put up with in the last century and a half?"

Before Michael could say anything, she poked his chest once more. Neither noticed the Executive Pod arriving on the park's lawn some fifty yards behind Bethany Anne. "They made me a *Gott Verdammt EMPRESS!*" she raged, her eyes blazing red. "And what were you doing, huh? Playing dead? Lying around on your ass, I bet!"

"I don't believe healing from a nuclear explosion is the same thing as lying around on my ass," Michael retorted. He was now being reminded of the other side of Bethany Anne, but then, one couldn't be attracted to fire without the possibility of getting burned. "While the Etheric Realm was pleasant when I woke up—"

"The Etheric Realm?" She arched an eyebrow. "That's where you were sitting around playing tiddlywinks?"

Michael saw John, Eric, Darryl, Gabrielle, and Scott come up behind Bethany Anne, and a couple of others had also exited the Pod. Akio let him know that he would greet the new arrivals, since it seemed Michael had his hands full.

He focused on Bethany Anne again. "The reintegration of my constituent atoms took a long time. Using the—"

She stopped him by poking his chest again. "Constituent atoms?" she exclaimed, her eyes flashing red. "Don't you go using big scientific words on me when I'm mad at you!" She looked him up and down. "I don't think you understand the concept of groveling!"

Eric whispered to John, "Did she slap him?"

"Tried," John whispered back. "Michael grabbed her hand before she could hit him."

Eric shook his head. "Should have just let it happen. That would have been enough." He flinched the smallest amount when Gabrielle smacked his arm. "See?" He pointed to his wife. "Just take the hit, and they're all better."

"I don't think that's in Michael's DNA," John said doubtfully as Ashur chuffed in agreement.

"So!" Bethany Anne retorted to the last thing Michael told her. "Think this is challenging you?" She shoved Michael off his feet. His body disappeared, and she put her hands on her hips. "Why don't you think about how to answer me politely while your ass sits in the Etheric until I come get it!"

Bethany Anne turned to her friends. "What?" she asked,

jerking a thumb over her shoulder as she stomped toward them. "He needs to understand how to act around me when I'm pissed."

Bethany Anne noted the exact moment their expressions changed to shock, and started to turn. She was halfway around when two large hands pushed her hard, throwing her toward her people.

She landed in the Etheric and rolled over to jump up, expecting an attack, but all she saw was Michael. He was ten feet away, his eyes glowing dimly. "You," he told her, "have been spoiled."

"*I'm* spoiled?" Bethany Anne screamed, her voice muted in the white mist. "You rank piece of fetid fish food!" She pointed a finger at him.

He interjected, eyebrow raised, "What, no 'fuck?' As in 'fucking rank piece of fetid fish food?'"

Bethany Anne twisted her head left and popped her neck, then did the same thing on the right. She whispered, "I'll feed you to the fucking fish, you gag-sacking dried-out cockroach-sodding bunghole-filler!"

Michael pursed his lips. "Does that mean you want it in both orifices?"

It took Bethany Anne only a microsecond to parse his question before her eyes flared red.

"I can*not* believe you just said that!" She walked to her right, staring him up and down. "I see you got the coat, but I've no idea why you chose the hat."

Michael turned with her, allowing his body a chance to limber up. He had heard Eric and John back on Earth talk about allowing the slap and while he could have accomplished it, that wasn't exactly who he was.

Nor was he the type of man Bethany Anne might need. He wasn't the type to be bowled over, which was why when she attacked, he pivoted and simply went down on one knee, lowering his head as she went past.

Surprised, she tried jumping, but her right foot just caught his leg and she stumbled. Falling forward, she stabbed the ground with one arm, kicking up into the air to pivot and turn around, landing on her feet.

Michael was standing there with his arms behind his back.

She shook her head. "You are a fucker!" she said as she walked up to him. She stabbed him in the chest again. "You *owe* me an apology!"

When he just looked down at her she twisted around, eyes flashing, took a step, and dropped out of the Etheric.

CHAPTER THIRTEEN

The entire group walked around the spot from which the pair had vanished in case they should suddenly reappear. John smiled at Akio and asked, "Did Michael upgrade?"

Akio shook hands with the men while Gabrielle hugged Yuko and Eve. The two of them introduced Gabrielle to Mark and Jacqueline, the young adults Michael had picked up in the old US.

Akio nodded slowly. "I think he is in much better control of his powers than when you last met him." He sighed. "This might take a while."

Just then Bethany Anne stepped out of the Etheric, her hair floating around her head. "*MEN!*" she shrieked. "Can't live with them, can't leave them on the side of the road when you're done with them! *URRRGH!*"

An arm reached out of thin air and pulled her backward, and her body disappeared.

A microsecond later Michael stood where she had been. "*Women!*" He harrumphed. He wiped off a sleeve and reached up to set his hat on his head, but a hand snaked out of the air, grabbed his hat, and disappeared. Michael whipped around. "She did *not* just take my fucking hat!" He took a step and disappeared again.

Everyone looked at the empty spot for a second and then resumed their discussions. Ashur let them know he was going to walk around for a few minutes, then go back to the shuttle.

Akio pointed toward the two people the guys didn't know. "Here, let me introduce you to Michael's wards."

"'Wards?'" Eric asked.

"Is that like kids?" John asked.

"Oh, goody!" Scott exclaimed, his eyes lighting up. He rubbed his hands together. "Does Bethany Anne know Michael has kids?"

"Give me back my *hat*!" Michael stormed into the Etheric, his head whipping around.

"What happened to your hair?" she asked as Michael spotted her. He strode in her direction as she walked backward, continuing to face him.

"My hat," he demanded, holding out his hand as he came toward her.

She put it behind her. "You didn't answer my question," she ground out. "What happened to your *hair*?"

Michael dematerialized and the hat was ripped out of her hands. Whipping around, she threw a right hook, catching Michael under his arm just as he raised it to put his hat back on his head.

He *whoofed* in pain as at least two ribs cracked before he disappeared out of the Etheric.

She dropped out of the Etheric too, only to catch a foot to her abdomen. She entered the Etheric again as she was in flight and crashed back to the ground. *"Gott Verdammt!"* She coughed as she got up, looking for him. "Where are you, you bastard? I'll rip your balls off."

A moment later Michael popped back into the Etheric, but before he could find her she ran right into him, head down, shoulders set. Michael's back cracked and he disappeared again.

This time Bethany Anne didn't follow him. She looked around, trying to see where he was.

Unfortunately she didn't think to look above, and Michael screamed "PILEDRIVER!" right before his elbow smashed onto the top of her head, tossing her out of the Etheric once more.

"OOOF!" he gasped when he hit the ground after she disappeared. Getting up, he scanned all around, then zipped forward a hundred yards, allowing the mist to hide him.

Soon enough, Bethany Anne's sweet voice called, "Come out, come out, wherever you arrrree." A second later she added in a slow, dark voice, "You toad-licking huphalump!"

Michael tried to gauge where she was, but needed a different angle. He faced where he thought she was and moved to his left.

"What, scared of little ol me?" she asked, her voice breathless.

Michael's lips compressed. She knew how to push his

buttons, even after all these years. "No," he replied, stepping quickly out of the way in case she came at him. "Just playing with the mouse I've found."

Soon enough Michael saw the red glow of her eyes and tore after her. His hat flew off as he ran forward, only to be shocked when the red he was following turned out to be two small red floating balls.

He never saw the punch.

Ejected from the Etheric, he hit the ground, and rolled over twice before he pushed up and disappeared once again from the park.

This time, Bethany Anne was standing not twenty paces away, hands on hips, eyes red. "Bring it," she hissed at him. "You bitch!"

Michael looked around for his hat, which was fifteen feet away, and he walked casually over to it and picked it up. After studying it, he wiped off a bit of grass. "Well." He placed it on his head and looked down to see all the grass stains. "That explains the clothes comments."

He turned to Bethany Anne and popped his neck. "Technically," he said conversationally, "My parents weren't married when I was conceived, so I can be called a bastard." As he started walking toward Bethany Anne his voice grew deeper and his eyes blazed red as his teeth elongated.

Bethany Anne heard him both with her ears and in her mind. "But no one calls me a *bitch!*"

>>**Oh shit,**<< ADAM remarked.

What he said, TOM agreed.

That was when Bethany Anne found out Michael had one button she might choose not to push again.

They went at it, blocking, kicking, and punching. Occasionally one or the other would be surprised and get tossed out of the Etheric, only to find the other waiting for them with a snide comment when they came back and started into it again.

"Seventeen," Mark said aloud as the ten of them glanced at the action. This time it was Michael who dropped out of the air some ten feet above the ground. His body slammed to the Earth, only to jump up a moment later and disappear once again.

"Is it only me, or is this a weird way to greet your lover after a long time?" Jacqueline asked. "I mean, Mark makes me mad, but I don't think that after a hundred and fifty years I'd fight with him like this."

Mark eyed his girlfriend. "That's good to know, I guess." Jacqueline elbowed him in the ribs, to the chuckles of the others.

"I was thrown by the kiss, actually," Eve put in. "I get update feeds from ADAM when Bethany Anne is here, and let me tell you—the fighting that's happening on the other side is dramatic."

"Probably just two alphas reasserting dominance." Gabrielle sighed. "Bethany Anne hasn't truly had to answer to anyone, and Michael still has that 'I'm the ArchAngel' thing going on." She tapped her lips. "Although I think he was probably ok until she tried to slap him."

"Michael is working to be a good man," Akio told her. "He's come far in becoming human again." He shook his head. "Allowing someone to slap him, even his love, isn't something he has worked on though, I can assure you."

Bethany Anne appeared twenty feet in the air and fell to the turf, rolling twice before she kicked off the ground. She was gone a half-second later.

"Eighteen," Eve announced.

"Who wants to bet on the number of times they show up before they kiss and make up?" Darryl asked.

"Twenty-seven," John replied immediately. "Closest wins, ties on either side of the guess go to the person who chose the smaller of the two numbers," he qualified.

Jacqueline scrunched her nose. "How does that work?"

"If one person suggests twenty-eight, and another thirty," John explained to the young werewolf, "and the number is twenty-nine, then twenty-eight wins."

"I'll take thirty-five," Scott piped up.

"Any reason you guys are going for odd numbers?" Eve asked.

Darryl shrugged. "Aren't they just numbers?" he answered. He was thinking about the last few times one or the other had appeared when Michael and Bethany Anne both slammed into the ground. Bethany Anne was still arguing as they rolled for a half-second before disappearing. "I've got twenty-three," Darryl told the group.

"Did she just call him a crusted bunghole of a space-zombie?" Mark wondered. "And that was nineteen."

"That's what I heard," Eric agreed. "What the hell, I'll go for the long shot. Forty-three."

Yuko asked, her voice slightly timid, "Are we betting on which one will finally give in?"

John scratched his chin as the ten of them watched

Bethany Anne appear, anger etched plainly on her face and her eyes flaming red. "That conceited gigantic—" she was yelling when Michael's arm snagged her around the waist and she vanished again.

"I believe she has a lot of anger to release," Gabrielle mused. "And Michael isn't allowing her to walk away and cool off."

"No." Akio added, "Also, he does not want to hold this discussion in public."

"She isn't going to like that," Gabrielle answered. "Well, the walking-away part. The not-in-public she won't care about."

Jacqueline smiled. "I'd love to know what they are saying on the other side," she admitted in a conspiratorial whisper. She turned to look to Eve. "Did you say ADAM was keeping you up to date?"

"Not exactly like that," Eve told her. "And I'll take twenty-five."

Akio looked at the android AI. "You have inside knowledge."

"That's ok with me," Gabrielle allowed. "Twenty-one."

"Wow, you're thinking she's almost done," Mark exclaimed. "Do you know both of them?"

"Yes," Gabrielle admitted, "although Michael was more of a boogeyman for most of my life."

"Which has been hundreds of years," Yuko told Mark as she pointed to Gabrielle. "Remember, this is Stephen's daughter."

Mark's mouth formed a silent "O."

Jacqueline's eyes narrowed. "That reminds me…where is this Tabitha female?"

Gabrielle turned to Jacqueline, and noticed the slight surprise in Yuko's eyes. Mark silently pleaded with his own eyes, imploring her, she felt, to minimize her answer.

She would have to get to the bottom of this, but Gabrielle had a rather solid suspicion. Jacqueline was obviously a werewolf, and Mark had the physical tells of a vampire.

Even if he *was* out in the sun.

Most female werewolves didn't like to share. Gabrielle jerked her thumb upward. "On the *ArchAngel*. Why?"

"Just curious." Jacqueline's eyes narrowed. "Is she coming down?"

"I'm sure she is," Eric piped up from behind her.

Gabrielle wanted to roll her eyes when she saw the blood—what little he had left, she guessed—drain from Mark's face. "Along with her boyfriend Peter." Gabrielle told them, trying to stave off a possible issue.

"Peter?" Mark interjected, relief in his voice.

"Yes," John answered. "The Queen's Guardians' leader."

Jacqueline's focus locked on John. "*The* Peter?" she asked, her excitement palpable. "The one the Queen saved?"

"Yes," John answered. "Did you know him?"

This time, it was Mark's eyes that narrowed in annoyance.

She shook her head. "No, but my dad told stories of Bethany Anne's saving him, and how he turned around. Hell," she gushed, pointing to each of them, "he told me about you too, John." She pointed to the others. "And Darryl and Scott and Eric."

"Who was your father?" Eric asked.

"Gerry," she answered.

"The Pack Council Leader Gerry?" John asked, and she nodded. "Damn! You obviously take after your mother."

Jacqueline opened her mouth to protest, but what came out was a chuckle. "Yes," she finally agreed. "My dad was a lot of things, but a fine-looking specimen?" She shook her head.

"Your dad wasn't ugly," Eric argued. "Perhaps not a ten, but not a two either."

There was a *woomph* as bodies hit the ground, but none of the ten even flicked an eye toward the noise.

"Twenty," Gabrielle commented.

"Dad would have appreciated your support," Jacqueline turned to Eric, "but even I know he was a solid six, maybe a seven if he shaved."

Darryl was going to ask where he was when the ten of them received a message.

We will be a while, Michael sent, followed by Bethany Anne's, **I've got some booboos to heal.**

Then the ten were alone.

"Did she mean," Gabrielle questioned everyone there, "that she had the booboos, or Michael had the booboos and she was going to make them better?"

No one spoke for a moment, thinking through what Michael and Bethany Anne had told them. "I'm not sure we will ever know," John replied.

Gabrielle shrugged. "Ok, pay up, bitches!" Gabrielle winked at Jacqueline. "I *won!*"

After five more minutes with no sign of Michael or Bethany Anne, Akio wondered aloud, "Does anyone want to meet Michael's cat?"

CHAPTER FOURTEEN

Etheric

This time it was quiet in the Etheric.

Michael was lying on the ground, his coat beside him, with Bethany Anne resting her head on his chest. "I am sorry," Michael finally broke the silence. "It took a long time for me to reconstitute enough to come back to consciousness. I think I reacted in fear for a while. To awaken was to feel the pain of the bomb eating my flesh away tick by tick. I was fleeing the bomb area in my Myst form when the explosion caught up to me. I could not tell you how long it truly was before I might have been whole, but I am pretty sure I would not have been back before your team left the solar system."

Bethany Anne sighed, thinking back to those times she had felt something in the Etheric. "You were there the whole time." She reached behind her head and ran a hand down his chest. "I think I might have been just as upset with myself for leaving you there."

"How were you supposed to know?"

"You dropped out where?"

"Colorado, near where the bomb went off."

She turned on her side, leaving her head on his chest, and stared at him as he looked into her eyes.

"What?" he asked.

"That's why I never found you." A tear slowly formed. "You were there, but you weren't solid. I could feel you, but I never found you…and I did look." She reached up and put a hand on his face to feel him again. "I promise you I looked."

Michael put his hand over hers. "You did what you had to do." He made a face. "Except that part about sending my casket into the sun. That wasn't necessary."

She pulled her hand away and slapped his chest, the sound loud in the silence of the Etheric. "You ass! I gave you a moving eulogy."

He grinned. "I know. It was beautiful." He reached down to caress her face. "I need to tell you this, and I'll say it again in front of everybody, but here goes…"

She looked up into his eyes, a tear of joy in one corner. "Bethany Anne, Matriarch of the Vampires…"

>>**Oh wow.**<< ADAM said. >>**He knows.**<<

Michael continued, his words giving her mind sweet peace. "I love you. I love the woman you were before I passed, I love the woman you were while I was gone, and I love the woman you are now. I accept any love you might still have for me, and I will love you forever more."

Bethany Anne, tears streaming, kissed his chest.

Michael continued. "I don't know our future, but know that I'll always be with you, through hell and back…"

Bethany Anne kissed another part of his chest, this time a little closer to his mouth.

"We will make it there together. I'll never forsake your *mmmphhhh.*" Michael quit talking when Bethany Anne's lips met his.

A moment later she came up for air. "Don't make me create real booboos to kiss." She reached for his shirt collar and ripped it down his chest. She had a red glow in her eyes as she licked her lips, her fangs growing. "I want you too bad for that!"

This time Michael wisely kept his mouth shut.

Michael looked down at his shirt, lifting one side and then the other to examine the rip. "Well, this won't be easy to hide," he said, chagrined.

Bethany Anne patted his stomach. "You wear it well, so flaunt it." She reached up to his head. "What really did happen with your hair?" she asked, playing with the quarter-inch stubble.

He turned, searching for his hat before walking three steps and picking it up. He dusted it off and put it back on his head as he explained, "Well, when I dropped out of the Etheric I was completely bald."

Bethany Anne frowned. "It's growing back slowly?"

"No," Michael admitted as he picked up his coat and shook it out. "It wasn't growing back at all until recently. Now it's growing back quickly, so I'm not complaining, but I was rather hoping you wouldn't arrive until it had grown back out," he admitted sheepishly as he put on his coat.

"Michael?" Bethany Anne stepped over and grabbed him by the chin, pulling him down for a kiss. "Are you vain?"

Michael sniffed, looking around. "I thought that was already clear!" he told her in a dignified manner before breaking into a grin. "Shall we fetch our friends and go up?"

Bethany Anne grabbed his hand and they stepped out of the Etheric.

"Where did everyone go?" Bethany Anne asked, looking around in the park.

>>**They are already on their way back,**<< ADAM replied.

How soon?

>>**Probably fifteen seconds, and then those staying or leaving can decide.**<<

"Incoming friends and compatriots in ten or so seconds." Bethany Anne grabbed Michael's hand. He was busy looking around at people taking photographs of the two of them.

"Did you ever get accustomed to the fame?" Michael asked softly.

Bethany Anne focused on what he was talking about for a moment.

"Some," she admitted. "It comes with the territory when you are the leader."

Hmmm. Michael rubbed his jaw as his eyes flicked to the sky, looking at the ships and then at the people around him again. They turned soon enough when someone mentioned the ships.

"I believe I liked it when the UnknownWorld was a little less obvious."

"I think," Bethany Anne watched the crew leave the old container box, "that secret is well and truly out."

A shadow passed over them and the two looked up when a lot of hands pointed into the air.

The craft that was coming down was sleek, black, and menacing, and sported a white female vampire logo on the side.

"That is one sexy bitch," Michael remarked as he watched the spaceship float down.

Bethany Anne leaned her head against his arm. "Shinigami probably heard that."

"Shinigami?"

"The AI who runs the ship," Bethany Anne replied. "She will like that you said that." Michael felt a small squeeze on his arm. "But if you say that about any other female—"

Michael chuckled. "I'm obstinate and arrogant, not idiotic and suicidal."

The ship stopped just short of the ground.

She patted his arm and they walked toward the ship. John and Eric had already pushed people back to give them room as they approached the stern ramp. "Good to know," she told him as they entered *Shinigami*.

"Holy…" Mark looked at Jacqueline, who was completely oblivious to his comment. She was staring out of the view screen at the massive ship as well.

"That's…" she started. She stopped for a moment before finishing her thought. "I understand why guys have inferiority complexes." She turned to Akio. "I'm feeling a little put in my place."

"What place?" Mark asked, returning his gaze to the ship. "She's been at this longer than you. Give yourself a little credit." He pointed to the ship out there. "Work hard, be handed a shit-ton of money and the objective of saving the world, and all that can be yours, too."

Jacqueline pursed her lips. "I think I got lucky with you."

"Mmhmm," he answered.

"You aren't listening to me, are you?" She raised an eyebrow. Akio glanced at Mark, who was staring at the video screen. He closed his eyes so he wouldn't watch the train-wreck about to occur.

"Mmhmm," Mark answered again.

"Does this outfit make me look fat?" she asked, her voice super-sweet.

"Mmhmm," Mark answered again. Her eyes narrowed as she inhaled. "But," he turned, winking at her, "I think you look sexy exactly the way you are, so what does it matter?"

Akio opened one eye. It flicked from Mark to Jacqueline, and then back to Mark before he opened the other eye.

This young man was smarter than Akio had given him credit for.

"I don't know whether to be upset with you for saying I'm fat or kiss you for saying you like me just the way I am," she answered. She put up a hand between them. "Don't be trying to lay a kiss on this," she waved it around her face, "until I figure it out."

Mark smiled to her. "The answer depends on whether you want the truth from me. Those ladies who are seeking the right answer, truth be damned, aren't helping their relationships. You asked if I thought that outfit made you look fat." His eyes went down her body and back up. "And it makes you look like you have an additional five pounds on you. But I know what's underneath—intimately—and I don't care what the clothes up top have got going for false advertising ."

"Kiss." She reached up to pull Mark's head closer. "Now you can look at that sexy bitch out there." Her eyes glinted just a little with moisture.

A voice rang out over the speakers in the ship. "I will accept that as a compliment."

Jacqueline put a hand over her mouth, "Oh my God!" she whispered, "did I just call the Queen a sexy bitch?"

"No," a voice that sounded remarkably like the Queen's answered. "You called *me* a sexy bitch, and I'll accept that as a compliment."

Both Jacqueline and Mark turned to Akio, who shrugged before he asked the ship, "Am I speaking with ArchAngel?"

"Yes, Akio," the voice replied as the Pod closed in on the ship. "Specifically I am ArchAngel II. I was made in my mother's image."

"*Hai*," he replied, dipping his head in a small bow. "It is an honor, ArchAngel."

"Likewise. My mother has worried about you, and she is happy to know you are safe." The three of them noticed one of the black X-wing vessels move into position beside them. "You will now have a guard with you at all times."

"Wait, why?" Jacqueline asked, seeing that more of the ships had been out there the whole time as they flew from Earth to the fleet surrounding the planet.

"Any time you are off-ship, the Queen wants enough firepower to 'lay waste to a shit-ton of idiots,' as she put it, if they dared try to harm you."

"Oh," she answered a bit meekly. "I thought it was to stop us from, uh…" She looked at Mark and then Akio. "Never mind."

"You will find, young Jacqueline," Akio told her as he watched the ships around them, "that the Queen is very protective of *all* her people." He glanced at the two fighters that flanked the ship, which had the Queen inside it as well. "Sometimes others can be very protective as well."

They slowed as their ship pierced *ArchAngel*'s field and slowly entered the massive bay, which was easily a hundred yards long and thirty high. Mark noticed that the ship they were on took up most of the bay.

He looked around, thinking that it was a good thing the people who had invaded Earth were *from* Earth.

The three disembarked, with Michael and Bethany Anne in the front. "Do not get too comfortable yet." Akio told the Were and the vampire. "We are here for some refreshments, and then we will catch another ride back to the planet."

A Yollin walked through a nearby hatch, joking with a human as they turned and headed down the bay.

Akio shook his head. This wasn't going to be a quick trip. He was about to push the two of them forward when the hatch opened again and a Leath stepped out and ran to catch up with the two from before.

The three watched the massive and fearsome alien grunting for a moment before the previous two turned and waved it forward. They waited until it had caught up, and then the three continued toward another ship.

A female's voice caught their attention. "What's the matter?" The three of them turned as Gabrielle, who was behind them, finished, "Cat got your tongue?" She winked at Akio. "This and more will be shown to you later. Let's keep moving."

Mark blushed as Jacqueline pulled him along, but he kept looking over his shoulder as the three hooked up some lines to the ship's belly.

CHAPTER FIFTEEN

QBS *ArchAngel II*, Orbiting Earth, Cafeteria Level Six

Jacqueline pushed her empty plate away from her. "I don't think I can eat another bite," she huffed as Mark walked up behind her, setting down a new plate plus a plate with a slice of chocolate cake next to it. "Except for whatever I'm smelling here." She pulled the second plate closer.

Lowering her head, she inhaled the scent of the cake and waved a hand negligently to Mark. "You may go and fetch yourself another one of these."

'That *was* mine," he told her, eyes amused.

"So?" She looked up, a smile on her face, "Consider it an object lesson for the course Food-You-Don't-Put-Down-Next-to-Your-Girlfriend 101." She picked up her fork and put the first bite in her mouth. The chocolate exploded with a few flavors she couldn't connect with Earth.

Groaning, she looked back at Mark, who was looking at what was left of his slice of cake. "I'll forgive you for not bringing me a second slice this time, because I was already stuffed." She blew him a kiss and smiled for all she was worth. "Thank you!"

Mark shook his head and headed back toward the line.

"I thought you were full?" Gabrielle asked Jacqueline.

"I was, but this smell just makes me want to hurt people if I don't have more cake," Jacqueline admitted, putting a hand up in front of her mouth to hide any teeth that might have chocolate on them.

Gabrielle frowned and reached over to the plate. Jacqueline had barely started to protest when her nose stung like a sonofabitch and her eyes started watering. "Wha di oo do to my noth?" she asked, both hands covering her face as she worked through her pain.

"I swatted you," Gabrielle answered, lifting the cake to her nose. "Oh, the chef put some Yollin winnomine in here." She placed it back in front of Jacqueline. "Don't act like you weren't about to growl or do something particularly disrespectful, and your nose should be fine in a moment," she thought for a second, "or two."

Jacqueline rubbed her nose and reached down to grab another bite of cake, eyeing the woman across the table.

Mark slid a new plate onto the table. "Here's another one for you, and here is mine. But I swear on an Intel I7, if you so much as try—" Mark's hand shot out, spearing Jacqueline's right wrist and pinning it to the table just inches from his plate.

She smiled at Mark as her left hand slowly grabbed the other cake plate and brought it back her way.

"A girl's gotta try sometimes," she told him, pulling her right hand back after Mark released her.

"Uh huh," Mark replied, sitting down and pulling his

cake toward him while keeping his eye on his girlfriend's hands.

New York City State, Old United States

"Daaaammn," Mark whispered. The three of them were going back down to Earth in something Gabrielle called a "low-level Executive Pod."

It was *plush*.

Akio sat back and enjoyed the seats as Jacqueline and Mark whispered between themselves about the "Ten-Thousand-Mile-High Club" behind him.

He considered explaining that they weren't ten thousand miles above the Earth, but decided to drop it. They were just playing and frankly, after everything they had been through since meeting up with Michael, he didn't begrudge it.

The fact that they had made it through as minimally affected as they seemed to have been was in itself a miracle.

He wasn't sure if they would have some sort of PTSD once they were safe, but he would make sure he spoke with ArchAngel to keep tabs on them once they left. PTSD was a thing from the past, and even vampires he had known throughout his life had been affected years later. These two seemed to have been helped by being around Michael and his radiant self-assurance.

Akio didn't let them know it wasn't self-assurance on Michael's part that they would all be ok, but rather acceptance that whatever would be would be, and a complete failure on Michael's part to clarify how they interpreted their feelings.

Akio had spent fifteen minutes with Bethany Anne, and those were some of the most precious he had experienced in his life to date.

Gabrielle had provided his men with an honorable way to surrender. Bethany Anne had shown him and his people honor as her guards, and now a team of hers would pull the massive amount of rubble off his men who were stuck on Earth and, fingers crossed, they would be waiting for him when the tons of rock were removed.

First their operations in Japan would have to be finished, though, and the fact that massive ships were flying around the world would need to become commonplace.

For now, the three of them were going back to New York one last time.

Mark didn't have any family he wanted to visit, but he did have a few restaurants he wanted to take Jacqueline to and in return, Jacqueline wanted to take Mark clothes shopping.

For him, of course.

Jacqueline took Mark through the park near Michael's home again just to see if anyone would come out and attack them, but she couldn't get anyone to bite.

A full day of shopping and eating later, the trio spent a nice night in a fancy hotel and took off from the hotel's roof the next morning.

But this time two of the fighters and one seriously large ship were waiting for them as they soared above the city, getting ready to head west.

· · ·

QBS *ArchAngel II*, Orbiting Earth

Giles nodded to John and Eric. "Hey, guys, Bethany Anne asked for me?"

"She did," John answered, eyeing the man. "Are you going to say anything arrogant, ignorant, or condescending?"

Giles raised his eyebrows. "Have you ever known me—"

"Since you were born, pipsqueak," John cut in.

Giles shrugged and nodded. "Fine, that's true. But have you ever known me to be *that* way?"

Eric turned in his direction, "Are you shitting me?" he asked, surprised. "Only since you could speak."

Giles rubbed a hand down his jacket. "But have you ever known me to be that way with *Bethany Anne?*"

"No," John admitted, "and that's why we are reminding you. I don't want to have to come in there and try to save your ass."

"Well, thank you!" Giles smiled.

"Don't thank him too much, Giles." Eric winked. "We don't like to clean up blood."

John popped Giles on the back, his smile sincere. "Have a good time, but remember the daughter doesn't put up with the same shit her dad does."

"Right." Giles nodded as John asked ArchAngel to open the door. "Hope to see you guys soon."

Giles entered the suite, the sound of the door sliding shut behind him making him feel as if he were entering the tiger's den—not that speaking with Bethany Anne was normally a dangerous proposition.

Unless you happened to have a mouth like his.

He wasn't deliberately annoying, but history, knowledge, and learning were his life. He usually had no filter when any of these subjects were in play.

His mouth just might cause his demise.

Inside the suite, the Queen was talking with a female and a small android.

He knew who they were, and his excitement bubbled over. "Yuko, Eve?" The three turned in his direction, and the Queen raised her eyebrow. Giles put up a hand. "My apologies. I shouldn't have interrupted you."

Bethany Anne nodded slightly. "Giles, you guessed correctly. Please meet Yuko and Eve. Yuko, Eve, please meet the son of Frank and Barbara Kurns and our own space archeologist, Giles Kurns."

As the three shook hands Bethany Anne continued, "He might be able to help you with the Kurtherian ship artifacts, which—"

Giles' eyes lit up. "You have artifacts from the Kurtherian race?"

Bethany Anne rolled her eyes to the ceiling, praying for patience. "Giles?"

He continued peppering Yuko and Eve with questions.

"*GILES!*" she barked. Giles jumped and turned to her. "Take your questions out of here. Yuko, please introduce Giles to Akio, Mark, and Jacqueline on the way out. They might have some insights, and introductions can help smooth things over. Giles, acquire transportation and go down to the planet with them when Yuko and Eve are ready."

"Certainly!" He put out an arm out to each of them. "Ladies?" he asked, his smile inviting.

Both Yuko and Eve shook their heads hesitantly, but they did accept his invitation and the three left her suite, chattering.

"Barnabas will be going with you!" she called, but the suite door shut right after and she wasn't sure they had gotten her message.

Old Denver (Former USA)

The Weres in the compound looked up when Terryl pointed to the sky.

Seventeen heads gazed upward and those on the nearby rooftops turned, their guns by their sides. One chose to raise his before a companion on the rooftop across the street yelled at him to put it down and to get off the roof for "being a damned fool."

Four airships were arriving. One was easily over a hundred feet long, and there were massive guns on the top and along the wings. There were two that looked like fighters, whose wings had an "X" design. They split off to circle the other two ships.

These weren't from Earth. No, everyone realized these were from the armada that had come back.

These were the Queen Bitch's ships.

The final ship was only about twenty-five feet long and continued toward the ground while the massive parent ship hovered some three hundred feet in the air.

Demitry, as the new Alpha of the clan, walked away from the protection of the main building toward the ship that had landed and was opening a hatch. It wouldn't do, Demitry thought, to look anything less than an alpha.

Except that anyone paying attention caught his slight stumble when he recognized the girl who stepped out.

"Shit," he mumbled, but he kept walking.

She was back.

The second person out of the ship was a day-walking vampire, but not the man Demitry had feared—not that it mattered. The third person to exit was a Japanese man, a vampire, and someone Demitry *had* heard of.

Akio.

Demitry stopped fifteen feet from the ship and nodded. That was as much respect as he was willing to give until someone forced him to bow. "Welcome, and peace be upon you in our home."

Jacqueline nodded after she had categorized all the threats she could see. "Hello. I am here to retrieve my father's remains."

Demitry raised an eyebrow and turned toward the rock cairn that marked the return of the Dark Messiah and the absolute power he had manifested when he had destroyed not only their own Alpha but three vampire hunters who had come to acquire Michael's blood.

Michael hadn't seen fit to share.

"We have not touched it." Demitry watched as the young lady and her…boyfriend, he guessed, walked together to the gravesite. He kept his distance from Akio too, who kept his eyes flitting from location to location.

Demitry put up his hands, signaling to the lookouts to stand down.

He was responsible for the pack, and if one of the fabled pair could destroy so much with just his powers and his pistols, how much more could his mate accomplish with her starships?

He had no intention of finding out. Akio was eyeing him. "I've commanded them to stand down," Demitry explained. "I don't want any misunderstandings with my people." He shook his head. "I offer my respect, and ask that you let me know if we can do anything for you."

Akio walked toward the alpha, giving him a small bow of respect in return as he approached. "It is our intention to treat you as we are treated," he told him. Akio looked around. "I believe the Queen will be pleased by your actions."

When Akio glanced at them, Mark was comforting Jacqueline as her shoulders shook. Her face was against Mark's shirt, no doubt getting it wet. "What are your challenges?" he asked the Alpha.

Demitry looked around and then at the massive ship over his head, which was big enough to cast a sizeable shadow on the ground. "Food, water, and power," he admitted, "not necessarily in that order."

"*Hai*," Akio nodded, lips pursed, then asked. "Clothes?"

"Those we have enough of." Demitry scratched his jaw. "But shoes and blankets?"

Akio reached to his shoulder, tapping something there and whispered softly enough that even Demitry's hearing couldn't make out most of the words. He did however catch "By request of the Queen's Bitch" and "supplies."

Akio continued looking around as he nodded in response to something Demitry could not hear. "*Hai*," was all he said before returning his gaze to Demitry. "Provide me the needed sizes of shoes, and we will have the rest delivered." He turned to the two young adults. They were still having a personal moment, so he turned back to Demitry. "You have kept her father safe. It is the least we can provide you."

Demitry turned to watch the girl and her mate and thought to himself, *I'll accept the offer, and there was no fucking way we were touching the cairn of a friend of the Dark Messiah.*

Jacqueline held Mark's hand, but she didn't feel the touch as she finished her short walk to where her father had been buried and covered in rocks. It had been a long time since she was here, and the emotions she thought she had buried rose up afresh, sensitive and painful. The tears started falling before she spoke a single word.

"Father…" she got out before she turned her head and buried it in Mark's chest, sobbing uncontrollably. Mark's arm came around her, holding her as she allowed herself the opportunity to grieve and release the pain through the tears streaming down her face to soak Mark's shirt.

Jacqueline reached up to wipe away the latest tears and sniffled, then turned back to the cairn in front of her. "You would be proud, Papa," she said before she lowered her eyes, allowing the tears dropping off her face to cascade down to start a small puddle by her feet. A couple of minutes later she breathed in deeply, wiping her eyes and taking an offered piece of cloth to blow her nose.

"I did it, Papa!" She breathed out heavily. "I followed Michael. I learned what it meant to fight for your people… for our people." She thought back to the battle in France with Sabine. "And for those I barely knew." She reached an arm around Mark and pulled him a bit closer. "I've got someone I want you to meet." Her tears started afresh, but this time she chose to talk through them. "God, how I wish you were really here to meet him." She held Mark tighter. "You would be proud, Dad. I caught me a good one, and I promise not to fuck it up."

"Hello, sir." Mark's voice surprised her. She looked up and saw the tears in his eyes. "My name's Mark, and I'd like to ask your permission to marry your daughter." He looked down at Jacqueline, who was staring at him with her mouth open in surprise. "That is, if she will have me."

Peace descended over the whole Pack at that moment and everyone's eyes turned to the two next to the cairn, who were kissing.

Those who were attuned could feel an extra presence around them before it dissipated, leaving everyone feeling just a bit better.

Later, Jacqueline watched as the ship above slid into place. The cairn—rocks, body and all—were lifted by an invisible field and pulled into the ship for transfer to, Jacqueline thought, the *ArchAngel II*.

Akio strode up to the two of them as they watched the cairn disappear into the ship. "We do not," he told Jacqueline as she dropped her eyes to him, "leave our own. His body will be moved to a casket."

"What would normally happen next?" Jacqueline asked.

"The Queen will ask you for your preference, but I can tell you that when she thought she had lost Michael, his casket was shot into the sun so his atoms could be distributed throughout the universe."

Jacqueline looked at the ship as it rose higher, waiting for them to leave. "Then that is where my father will go."

CHAPTER SIXTEEN

<u>Abandoned Airfield, One Hundred Fifty Miles North-Northwest of Chengdu</u>

Giles stood over one of the crates Yuko and her team had liberated from Chinese soil.

"So how come you haven't opened them all?" he asked.

Eve glanced across at Yuko across the pile of parts she was cataloging. "It's like having a nerdier version of Mark around." She chuckled, putting her hand over her face to hide her giggle.

Yuko couldn't help herself and spluttered out a giggle, too.

Giles' face turned pink. "Really? I'm nerdier than Mr. Computer-Head?"

Yuko nodded earnestly and Sabine piped in her agreement from the other side of the crates.

Knowing he wasn't going to win this discussion, Giles turned his attention back to the three unopened crates. He started pulling at a strange lid while making prolonged grunted noises.

Yuko chuckled and moved toward him. "Let me help," she said, bending down, flipping the catch, and removing the lid effortlessly. "What kind of archeology did you say you specialized in?" she asked, slightly mocking him with her eyes, if not her tone.

Giles grunted something unintelligible and peered into the box. "Things are usually a little more complicated than a catch," he told her, trying to recover the part of his ego that had been flicked away with the lid. "We have to break codes and solve puzzles normally."

"Which was obviously what you were attempting when you heaved at the lid, yes?"

"Well, erm, quite," he agreed, his mind now firmly on the contents of the box. He started hauling pieces out, examining them and then putting each aside as he dove back in for the next piece.

Yuko moved to another box to help Eve with the arduous task they had committed to. "You know, he kind of reminds me of a kid opening Christmas presents," she said ever-so-quietly.

Eve nodded, simulating the human mannerism. "Actually he reminds me of the previous century, when men had hundreds of television frequencies to explore."

Yuko cocked her head, confused.

Eve continued, "You know, where they had that controller and sat in front of the screen all night? They would flick through one channel after another, and the joke was always that they didn't want to know what was *on* the TV. They wanted to know what *else* was on the TV."

Yuko snorted, and quickly covered her mouth and nose again.

Giles looked up, bewildered. "You know, it isn't fair that you two are always ganging up on me. I'm new to this planet and you're...merciless."

Yuko straightened her face. "You're right, and I'm sorry. It's been a long time since we had someone around we could be so merciless toward. Forgive us?"

Giles pulled out another device, his attention captured. "Yes, yes, of course," he muttered absently, turning the object in his hands. It was a strange metallic disc of some sort. Eve noticed it only because of the reaction Giles seemed to have toward it.

He stared at it for several seconds, turning it over now and again as if captivated by it psychically. It certainly wasn't an object of beauty...which was why it seemed odd.

After a few minutes he snapped out of his somnambulistic state, set it down with the other things he'd taken from the crate, and continued his investigation.

"Got anything interesting?" Eve queried.

Giles shook his head, one arm searching in the crate. "Nothing that I understand...*yet*," he called back.

Suddenly the massive hangar door shuddered and Barnabas appeared. He walked briskly toward them, covering the length of the building in moments. "I'm afraid we have a problem," he announced. "I'm sensing movement out there, and I believe it's on the approach. What kind of defenses do we have here?"

Yuko and Eve blinked at each other and Eve responded, "We have ourselves. This hangar was our nearest tactical option. As for defenses, that was it. We don't have any heavy artillery here since you sent the others away."

Barnabas' face bore a mixture of expressions. It was as

if he were trying to convey dismay, and yet in his eyes there was a glint of hunger.

Yuko recognized it. It was the same hunger that Sabine had shown for destroying things. It was the same hunger she'd felt within herself since her Michael-awakening. "Such a shame we'll have to go out there with nothing but our Jean Dukes and our swords," she said casually.

Giles paled, his eyes flitting between Barnabas, whom he knew, and the young Japanese woman, whom he did not.

"Don't worry," Yuko told him. "Archaeologists can sit this one out. Just stay inside and keep low. She waved at the crates. In fact, if you stay low amongst this lot, you'll probably be pretty well protected."

Yuko and Sabine had already trailed after Barnabas, who was almost back to the door again. Yuko spoke with Sabine, who nodded her head and turned around as Yuko continued.

Giles looked at the mess of parts and devices, still processing that they were under attack. "But what if they come for this stuff?" he called.

"Don't let them take it!" Yuko called back to him as she continued out the door, Eve catching up to her.

Giles shook his head, muttering to himself. "Don't let them take it. And if they throw a missile my way...what am I supposed to do? Catch it in my *teeth*?"

Suddenly all the extra training seemed futile. If he survived this, he promised himself he would most certainly find a way—by hook or by crook—to make sure that he didn't feel this incapable *ever* again.

Yuko and Eve stepped out of the hangar. Sabine had stayed in the hangar with Giles to repel boarders. They could see the chopper approaching in the distance even before their enhanced hearing picked it up.

But they had more immediate problems. Coming up past the old fence on the outskirts of the base were scores of soldiers in Chinese gear with blasters and guns and all kinds of equipment.

"Apparently someone in the Chinese hierarchy didn't get the message." Barnabas scratched his face. "Good."

"Could be they got bought out." Eve started moving in the direction of the box's cabin. "I need my accessories for this one," she said, moving as fast as her legs could carry her.

Yuko nodded, preparing herself by mentally picturing the ones she would obliterate first.

This was going to be bloody.

Very bloody.

Barnabas was ahead of them, his Jean Dukes drawn and the sword on his back ready if anyone got close enough for him to use them.

He stood poised. Powerful.

Yuko didn't know how well he fought these days. It had been a while and it was not the kind of thing one tended to discuss. "Hey," she began, coming up to him, "How was the last century and a half for you? And by the way, how up-to-date are your annihilation skills? Was that Ranger thing just an honorary appointment?"

She shook her head. *FOCUS!*

Whatever the answer, some of these bodies were going to get past him so she needed to be ready. The fate of those crates, and therefore the Earth as they were trying to leave it, was at stake.

Yuko drew her sword and adjusted her grip deliberately.

The first few soldiers came into range of Barnabas' pistols. *Pop. Pop. Pop-pop. Pop. Pop pop….*

Heads exploded one by one. Barnabas picked them off almost as gracefully as Sabine would have.

His finger squeezed the trigger, moved the pistol a tiny amount, and squeezed again.

It was a symphony of destruction.

The soldiers kept coming, wave after wave. Barnabas was dancing, never in the same spot, as the soldiers fired toward him.

Twice she had to move to avoid bullets heading in her direction. Once she saw his coat flip hard in the wind, a bullet having certainly plowed through it.

The chopper was nearly upon them, and Yuko glanced in Eve's direction. She was fitting her missile launcher onto her arm, but wasn't ready yet.

Yuko drew her Jean Dukes and waited for it to come into range. Meanwhile, unbeknownst to her, Barnabas already had it in range and had fired five shots strategically into it.

BOOM! The fuel tank erupted in fire, which rained down metal and destruction and rotating blades that flew across the airfield and sliced through anything in their path...which happened to include a number of the Chinese soldiers.

Yuko lowered her weapon and shrugged. Worked for her.

Meanwhile, since Barnabas had taken time out to drop the chopper, several men were nearly upon him. She started to move forward, but then she saw the glint of his blade as he deftly removed it from the sheath in his back.

He wasn't a target of the other guns, at least at the moment.

What followed was almost a dance, with the razor edge of his sword glinting beautifully in the sun and then being dulled by the red of the blood as it cut through its victims.

Blood splattered one way, then the other, falling in an ornate pattern on the asphalt around him as he stepped and turned and whipped the sword around, taking out anything that came within arms' length of him.

Yuko watched in awe. Michael and Akio weren't the only ones who were able to dial the level of carnage to eleven.

At one point he even pulled his Jean Dukes again and took out two soldiers who were making a break around the side of the hangar toward the crates.

It took several minutes for the carnage to end, but when it was done nothing moved.

Barnabas waited, immobile, casting a silent shadow over a couple of fallen bodies.

For effect? she wondered. *Or was he catching his breath?*

Nope. He was enjoying the moment!

He lifted his gaze to meet hers…and smiled.

That was the look of a man who was *really* enjoying his job.

Now she understood why he had sent the others away.

He hadn't wanted to share the fun.

Eve and Yuko strode purposefully back into the hangar and swept Sabine with them as they headed for the crates.

"Ok, Geek-boy, we need to wrap this operation up," Yuko announced.

Giles poked his head up from behind the crates, his glasses askew and his hair disheveled.

"You ok?" she asked, frowning at his strange appearance.

"Erm, yes, yes. All ok. Nearly ended up getting killed, but apart from that…"

Yuko glanced around, confusion evident in her voice. "But no one got in."

"There were guns firing out there!" he protested, pointing toward the open doors.

Yuko rolled her eyes. "Let's get you back to the ship," she suggested. She and Sabine started packing the pieces back into the crates. "We can do all this up there." She glanced at him once more. "And perhaps we need to let you blow a little steam off; get this fight out of your system."

Giles scrambled to his feet and straightened his glasses. "Righty ho. If you think that's best then," he said, hastily joining them in returning the pieces to the crates.

Eve had an idea. "I can bring the box in here," she told Yuko. She headed over to the hangar doors, and after a little struggling managed to get them to open wide enough.

Meanwhile, Barnabas had cleaned his sword and

composed himself. "May I be of assistance?" he asked Eve as he strode into the hangar.

Eve shook her head and gave him her best grin. She glanced at the array of bodies he'd left behind. "I think you've done more than a day's work already."

Barnabas smiled and bowed slightly. Then, without another word he headed back into the hangar to join the others.

Giles looked up from his trinkets to see Barnabas approaching, as cool as anything, and then he saw the carnage outside. "My goodness, it's like Devon all over again!" he exclaimed, slightly horrified.

Yuko frowned. "Devon? England?"

Giles shook his head, his eyes fixed on the scene just outside the hangar doors. "No, Devon-you-really-don't-wanna-know."

Yuko nodded once. "Right then," she said turning to Barnabas. "Nice job out there. You handled that...well," she paused, then finished wryly, "single-handedly."

CHAPTER SEVENTEEN

Abandoned Airfield, One Hundred Fifty Miles North-Northwest of Chengdu

Eve, Yuko, and Sabine were busy doing the heavy lifting and getting the crates into the black box.

Barnabas was back to being characteristically reserved and well-mannered.

Giles, meanwhile, was being characteristically vacant, watching nothing as the ladies did all the work.

"Walk with me," Barnabas said quietly to Giles, and headed into a darkened corner of the hangar.

Giles followed obediently. "'Sup, BB?" he jested, trying to lighten the mood.

Barnabas glanced back at him disapprovingly.

"Ok. Sorry, erm…Barnabas," he corrected himself.

Satisfied, Barnabas started climbing the stairs that led to a viewing gallery. Giles looked at the structure nervously. "You think that's safe?"

"Probably not," Barnabas retorted, continuing to climb.

Feeling like he had no choice, Giles cautiously placed

his foot on the first step and grabbed the handrail. It felt stable enough, so he followed Barnabas.

When they arrived at the top, Giles was breathing a little harder than usual although Barnabas showed no signs of exertion. He looked out over the hangar floor, watching the girls load the alien materials.

"There are some things you might not yet appreciate about Michael," Barnabas started.

Giles shoved his hands in his pockets. He saw where this was going. This was a conversation to formally warn him to behave around the ArchAngel, just as Lance had taken him aside about his behavior around the Empress.

"I think you're misunderstanding me," Barnabas said, reading his thoughts. "This is related, but more about how honor is important to the man. He doesn't tolerate insubordination, lack of respect, or stealing."

Giles swallowed hard as Barnabas focused his attention directly on him like an interrogation lamp. "I, er...don't know what you m—" he started to say.

Barnabas lowered his eyes to Giles' jacket. "In your pocket," he said simply.

Giles quickly reached in and pulled out the shiny metallic object that had captivated him before the disturbance and ensuing slaughter.

"Um…" He looked at the object and at Barnabas. "I can explain," Giles started again.

Barnabas' gaze stopped him. "No need. I don't care. What I *do* care about is the dishonesty, and what Michael will do to you when he finds out. And notice I say when...not if. In case you haven't already figured it out, you're surrounded by mind-reading, Etheric-bending beings now. You have to be cleaner than clean."

Giles hung his head solemnly. "I'm sorry. I was just going to keep it separate so I could research it some more when I got back to the ship. If it was stowed away in the crates I'd have to get access and the paperwork…"

His voice tapered off.

Barnabas' eyes softened. "I understand, but you need to come clean. Tell someone. Report it. Log it. You're part of a team now, and if you want your team to trust you, you *have* to stop pulling this kind of shit."

He sighed and rested his hands on the railings, noticing that the structure was rather more precarious than he had originally thought. "You're not a kid anymore, Giles. You're going to need to start acting more responsibly if you're going to continue to operate within the Federation. Tough times are coming. Big changes…"

Giles felt a shudder run through his spine. It was as if Barnabas were being prophetic. "Ok. I'll let Eve know now…" he promised, turning to leave.

"I'd take that other staircase down," Barnabas suggested, nodding in the other direction from where they had come up.

Giles, already on edge, didn't question it. No way was he going to take a chance twenty feet above the concrete floor.

He turned carefully and walked gingerly but as fast as he dared to the other staircase and headed straight down to Eve, who was lifting one of the crates.

Barnabas shook his head, chuckling inwardly to himself as he watched the man walk away from him.

"Kids," he muttered, shaking his head.

After a moment he jumped over the rail, barely flexing his knees as he landed twenty feet below, and headed outside again.

He could hope someone would be stupid enough to attack once more. Unlikely, but he could hope.

QBS *ArchAngel II*, Orbiting Earth

Bethany Anne was walking with Michael as they headed out of her suite and toward the docks. "A real ass-kicking date, is it?"

"I believe it might be," Michael agreed. "We know where the last person is who worked against Akio, Yuko, and Eve to get the Kurtherian parts. He set up a hit against the location they were stored in."

"That stuff that was left over when I killed their leader?" Bethany Anne asked.

"The very same," Michael agreed. "We have a location and a name—Kuro," Michael answered. "I'm not expecting it to take too long."

"Why?" Bethany Anne asked, her eyes narrowing.

"The last two individuals Akio and I went against were pretty low-grade," Michael answered as the two of them headed down another hallway. He looked around. "Where are John and Eric and the rest?"

"I told them to go watch over Bobcat, William and Marcus on a beer run. I don't think we need backup, do you?" She grinned mischievously.

Michael shrugged. *Whatever makes her happy.*

Five minutes later the duo were heading down toward the planet in the *Shinigami.*

"Queen?" Shinigami's voice sounded, sounding so much like her own that Michael did a double-take. They were lounging on the soft couches on the bridge.

"Yes?"

"The Bitches and Team BMW are leaving as well. Should I let them know where we will be?"

"Nope." Bethany Anne shook her head. "Those guys need some down time. I'll find something for them to do later."

Ten minutes later, or ten seconds—if Michael went by how it had felt—the two of them were hovering a mile above the location of the final straggler from their last operation. Michael had Shinigami crack the door and switched to Myst, then grabbed Bethany Anne and swept down through the night toward the last of the group who needed a healthy dose of killing.

This is beautiful, she commented. *I forgot what flying with you was like.*

Almost two hundred years, he replied wistfully. *And she forgets the fun times?*

Bethany Anne chuckled. *You know I will punch you for that, right?*

Michael chose to not answer as he swept around the two-story building. It looked like it was maybe five thousand square feet aboveground, and if this person was like his partners it would have some wonderful dungeon areas and underground exits as well.

He found an opening by the front door and solidified the two of them inside the first receiving room. It had beautiful grey stone flooring, and elegant walls done in a greyish green with Japanese paintings adorning them.

No doubt priceless.

Michael and Bethany Anne looked around. "Good thing Sabine isn't here," he murmured. When Bethany Anne raised an eyebrow he explained, "A woman we saved over in France. She has become very good with her guns—preternaturally so." He pointed to the paintings. "But she has a fetish for destroying artwork."

"Why *hello!*" a man's voice said as the speakers above them crackled to life. "I was not expecting you, but this does not surprise me."

Keep him talking, Michael sent to Bethany Anne.

Seriously? She pulled out her Jean Dukes when Michael disappeared. *I've got to listen to Adam Asswipe here?*

Just encourage his monologue, Michael sent. *We might get done with this quickly!*

Fine! Bethany Anne smiled at the camera she found up in a corner.

She waved her gun barrel in a circle. "I don't suppose you would provide me with a description of all of this shit between me and you, would you?"

The dry voice came back, "Normally I wouldn't. However," his voice rose just a bit, "you are now in my little shop of horrors. I've been paying attention to you paranormals for years, and whether you are a vampire or a werewolf, I've built just the tool I need to kill you dead."

He coughed, then continued. "Since I am giving out hints, tell me…are you a vampire or a werewolf?"

Bethany Anne's eyes glowed red and her fangs descended, "Don't you dare get the species wrong!"

"Oh, very good," he replied. "I see your much-vaunted lover has left you."

"He's annoying like that." Bethany Anne sighed heavily, "If one of us, you or I, is about to die soon…"

"You," his voice came back, cocky.

"Fine." Bethany Anne worked hard to stop her eyes from rolling out of her head. "Me, then. What am I facing?"

"Only the best that my brains and money could buy to protect me from abnormals such as yourself. I've spent the last twelve years planning in case one of your kind came for me."

He paused for a moment. "I am, I assure you, prepared."

I doubt it, Bethany Anne thought. *And if Michael doesn't kill this dick soon, I'm going to have to…*

Then she smiled. "Oh, hey, Michael? If you can hear me, I'm getting randy again, but I'd hate to have to wait for you to kill this asshole. It might cause me to—

A scream of pain, then the sound of gurgling blood. *That was tragic,* Bethany Anne thought as she checked her fingers. At that moment, the doors opened and screaming men came into her room.

Seven seconds and two bullets to the chest armor later, there were twelve dead security guards lying in their own blood around her.

Michael's voice was soft and sexy as he spoke over the security system. "He might have wanted to get his security system checked. I can't find anyone else alive in the building at this time. Does blood make you feel cold, or hot?"

Bethany Anne licked her lips, looking dead into the camera under the assumption that Michael was in the control room. The dead asswipe they had come here to kill was probably on the floor. She grinned. "Hot, Mr. Vampire Man. Very, very *HOT.*"

Half a second later Michael reappeared right in front of Bethany Anne, causing her to catch her breath as he swooped her into his Myst and went to the top of the building.

There was a very fine small apartment up there, and he happened to know the owner wasn't going to need it.

Ever.

Yokohama, Japan, Yokohamakeon (Park)

The Pods landed in the park. The same park that had been the landing spot of their black box numerous times over the last several weeks.

Giles bounded out, looking around him at the sunshine, sky, and gardens.

"This... This is *amaziiiiing!*" he cooed. "Is this really what Earth was like when Mom and Dad were here?"

Eve had already stepped out after him. "Pretty much. At least similar. Of course, they spent their time on the other side of the planet about a third of the way around from here, but that's not really habitable now."

Giles was in awe.

Yuko stepped out of her Pod. "So, what do you want to see?"

Giles suddenly stopped turning and fixed his eyes on Yuko. "I'm a space archeologist. Anything. *Everything.*" His face exploded into the brightest smile Yuko had seen in a long time.

She couldn't help but be amused as she subconsciously mirrored his expression. "Don't we need to go find some old places with ruins and stuff?" she teased.

"Yuko," Giles said, suddenly very serious. "I come from a society that has thousands of planets light years apart. Space archeology is a vibrant living science. Once upon a time it meant studying ruins, but now it's all about the study of civilizations, alive or dead. So much about the past foretells the present and the future. This city is a living, breathing testimony to that. Show me anything, and I will make a pretty good guess as to its past and its future."

Eve asked, "Seriously? You have that much data in your brain?" She glanced at Yuko for confirmation that this could possibly be true.

Giles gave his cocky, youthful grin. "You'd be surprised. Getting through higher education is pretty intense these days, especially the interplanetary courses like Space Arch and Anth."

Yuko took a deep breath, not sure if she believed everything he was selling, and tried again. "So, what should we show you then? The Senate?"

Giles lifted his arms upwards and then dropped them. "Sure. Let's take a look."

Yuko started fiddling with her handheld device, sending messages.

"What are you doing?" Giles asked, peering over her shoulder.

"Just making sure we get access when we get there."

"Huh?"

"Oh yeah," she said casually, mocking his cocky intonation. "I'm the Diplomat. Friends in high places. We'll be getting the behind-the-scenes tour." She grinned.

"Well…" Giles coughed in his throat. "You're kinda handy to have around," he admitted.

Eve giggled. "Even more so in a fight, especially these days."

Yuko visibly shriveled in embarrassment.

Giles looked impressed. "Oh yeah?" He eyed Yuko, wondering if his newly acquired skills could match hers.

Eve nodded. "Yeah, she's really gotten her Kill Bill on since Michael came back from the dead."

Giles' demeanor shifted. He looked slightly nervous, but nodded. "All righty, then. Good to know."

"Shall we?" Yuko suggested, indicating the two Pods they had just hopped out of.

"We should," Giles agreed, pleased he hadn't challenged her to a little sparring. "I'll ride with Eve. She can give me the low-down on your new style of diplomacy," he added, pretending to be more unnerved by her lethality than he actually was.

Yuko smiled sagely. "I'm sure she will tell you everything you care to know," she said as she hauled herself back into the Pod.

Giles scurried in after Eve, glad for the flight time to absorb the new pecking order.

CHAPTER EIGHTEEN

<u>Senate House, Tokyo, Japan</u>

On arriving at the Senate building, Yuko had been given free access as if she were the Queen of Japan. Giles kept thanking his lucky stars he hadn't been too cocky with her.

Something told him that Eve had refrained from bragging too much about Yuko's sword skills.

Still, there was fear, and there was respect.

Clearly all the people who they had encountered at the Senate had great respect for Yuko.

After their special tour, the threesome stepped out of the front of the building and ambled down the steps.

"Wow. Well, fascinating architecture," Giles commented politely.

Yuko smiled. "I don't know about you, but I was bored out of my skull."

Eve nodded her head with each downward step. "Me too."

Giles politely remained silent.

Yuko continued, "In fact, that tour guide…" She shook her head. "I think if I hadn't been the one to arrange the tour I might have been inclined to take my sword out!"

Eve sniggered. "That would have done wonders for future relations between the local government and the Tech Palace!"

Yuko winked at her. "True, but hey, it's not as if we're going to be here much longer."

A jarring sadness lingered in her words as the three reached the bottom of the steps and headed out of the main gates.

Eve filled the silence. "Yes. This is true."

Giles, finding his balls, decided to change the subject. "Sooooooo…" he started slowly and comically, "now that we've escaped the epic boredom of the Senate, what else is there in this town?"

Eve brightened suddenly. "We could show you the Tech Palace."

Yuko nodded excitedly. "It's a tech entertainment empire we built, mostly just for fun."

Giles stroked his chin. "Hmm. Yes, it would be good to see these folks being entertained in their natural habitat. Although…isn't there something a little less, er…cultivated?"

Yuko tilted her head. "Cultivated? How do you mean?"

"I mean…a little more…*wild?*" Eve was still confused. Giles tried again. "Like if I said, show me somewhere that is representative of your people at their best and their worst, where would you take me?"

Yuko grinned. "I know *exactly* the place!"

Giles eyed her curiously, but she wouldn't give anything up.

Eve just shrugged.

The Pods arrived right on cue, and the three clambered in. This time Giles sat with Yuko to try to discover where they were going.

Three Black Eagles flew with them to their next destination.

Golden Gai, Shinjuku, Tokyo, Japan

Yuko had a spring in her step as she led the way through the sweltering streets of the Shinjuku quarter of Tokyo. The humidity in the air was making her hair frizzy, even though it was normally quite straight.

Eve kept pace with her human friend, twisting and turning through the rabbit warren of streets as if they'd navigated this route a hundred times before.

If they had cared to admit it they might have divulged that information...but Yuko was hoping that word didn't get back to Akio and the leadership that they had spent so much time on Earth not just patiently waiting for a call from the sensors at the Colorado base where Michael had been blown into oblivion.

Although she frankly doubted Bethany Anne would care. For her it was more about decorum.

Giles had to make an effort to keep up, despite his longer legs. Still, captivated as he was by the sights, scents, and sounds the clubbing quarter offered, complaining about the pace was the furthest thing from his mind. "This is more like it!" he exclaimed with glee to no one in particular.

Yuko slowed her pace as they neared their destination. "We need to get you a drink *stat*," she said forthrightly.

"Great!" He glanced at Eve, suddenly suspicious.

"You're good with sake, right?" Yuko continued, her eyes darting around the street that was about to open onto a square.

"'Soy-kee?'" Giles repeated. "Erm, yes. I love it!" he lied.

Yuko inwardly rolled her eyes, but kept her face clear. "Great!" She flashed a grin at him before swiftly making her way through the nearest door on the street.

From outside it looked like little more than a converted house, but the innards had been gutted to make an open-plan kind of setup.

Pushing her way through the crowd of young energetic party goers, she took advantage of her lack of height to get to the bar.

She motioned to the barman, who seemed to recognize her, waving two fingers. In short order he produced two glasses and filled them with a clear liquid. She paid with her charge card, then grabbed the glasses and ducked back out to rejoin Eve and Giles, who had been watching her.

Yuko handed one to Giles and motioned for him to down it.

"What about Eve?" he asked, offering his to her.

"She can't," Yuko mouthed.

Eve opened her mouth. "Nowhere for it to go!" she shouted over the music. She made a sad face and then gave him her best pout.

Giles mirrored her pout in sympathy, then Yuko nudged him to make him drink.

He downed the small shot and his eyes flew wide.

Eve chuckled as he started choking and gasping for breath, throat burning.

"Oh my..." He coughed, looking around for someone to help him back to health, but all he could see were two women who hid their smiles behind their hands before they went back to speaking with their friends.

Eve clapped her hands, giggling, while Yuko, with a little more sympathy, patted him on the back. "Ok, this is just the warmup. Next place..." She slapped her empty glass on a nearby crowded high table and marched toward the door.

"Next place?" Giles echoed, suddenly concerned. He turned to ask Eve a question, but she was no longer there. Instead, she was disappearing behind Yuko onto the street.

He did a double-take, realizing that both girls had something of a rhythmic swagger in their step, as if moving to the music.

He found somewhere to put his glass and followed them. "Oh, hell. What have I gotten myself in for?" he muttered, pushing quickly through the crowd. He didn't want to get lost in this strange place.

Because that would be embarrassing as hell.

***

Back out on the street, the quarter seemed to vibrate with color and neon lights.

Groups of youths walked the streets, each with their

own subculture identification. Some would have bleached blond hair, others with colors and hair extensions. Some wore bizarre outfits, and others something reminiscent of torn jeans.

Many had strange luminescent clothes and bangles that seemed to float through the twilight streets on their own.

He tried hard to take it all in, one cohort of tribal culture after another, one fascinating-looking bar after another, while trying not to lose sight of Yuko and Eve.

Eventually, just past a cordoned-off shrine, the girls came to a halt.

Giles caught up with them, perspiration mixing with the humidity and dampening his skin. "What is it?" he asked, confused and already a little tipsy from the single shot of sake.

Weren't his upgrades enough to handle this stuff? he wondered as he looked around.

"There," Yuko told him, pointing to another club down the little alleyway.

Outside were animals. Or to be more precise, people dressed as animals. Lions, tigers, bears, cats.

Lots of cats.

And even a dinosaur, if Giles' eyes were to be believed.

He started chuckling. "Well, I did ask for local wildlife." He was completely delighted with the whole adventure.

Eve grinned at him. "And we *always* deliver."

"Yes. Yes, it would appear so," he agreed wholeheartedly.

"Ok, then. Shall we?" Yuko said, striding off without waiting for an answer.

Eve was a step behind her.

"But I'm…" Giles protested, following several paces behind and jogging to catch up. "I'm a little under-dressed for this!"

Eve was still grinning. "Don't worry, no one will notice."

For some reason Giles wasn't reassured as he trotted after them.

CHAPTER NINETEEN

Club Wire, Shinjuku, Tokyo, Japan

A skinny dancing elephant sashayed past the table. Giles watched it move, mesmerized by the curvaceous shape of the girl under the costume.

Yuko poured some more sake into his glass. "Drink!" she instructed.

Without taking his eyes from the dancing elephant, Giles brought the glass to his lips and took a sip, turning in his chair to examine a couple of cat-people who had caught his eye.

Dry ice obscured a lot of his view and lasers reflected off it, creating a surreal feel.

Blacklights illuminated anything that was made of the right material—including his teeth, much to Eve's amusement.

Eve shuffled closer to Yuko to be heard above the music. "You seem distant."

Yuko waved a finger near her ear and shrugged, as it to blame the music.

Eve raised one robotic eyebrow very deliberately, then lowered her voice to the minimum possible decibel level. "That's not an excuse," she said flatly. "I know you can hear me and I can hear you equally well, so come on. What gives?"

Yuko narrowed her eyes. *When in the last hundred and fifty years had Eve become so damn perceptive? And persistent?*

"It wouldn't have anything to do with a certain Inspector, would it?" Eve pressed.

Yuko had lowered her gaze to her drink, but now reluctantly dragged it up to look at Eve. She nodded slowly.

Giles had started talking to the pair of cats who had caught his eye and a guy in a latex dragon suit, so Yuko felt cornered. It was indeed inappropriate to talk about it without excluding him.

She sighed in surrender. "I just can't stop thinking about him," she admitted slowly.

Eve nodded her head comically, almost in glee, then took a second to compose herself. "Not that I have a lot of experience in this kind of thing, but I do know from watching relationships play out in the stories in the archives that this is the part where you get your finger out of your ass and go find him!"

Yuko's expression was horrified.

Eve sniggered and poured her friend another drink. "Come on, you guys were made for each other. Goodness knows why you chose to walk away from him."

"I didn't have a choice. He was in danger!" Yuko protested.

Eve gave Yuko her best best-friend look and patted her hand mockingly.

Yuko slapped her arm.

Eve continued with her diatribe. "My analysis says it would be an easy story to tell, but that's far from the truth."

Yuko started to protest, but Eve raised her finger to silence her. "Firstly, *if* that were true, as soon as the threat on the hangar had been neutralized and Akio gave us the all-clear on the other loose ends you would have been over there like a shot."

Yuko opened her mouth again, only to be silenced by Eve's raised finger.

"Secondly, if that were the only reason, you would have hunted down whoever it was who came after you in that restaurant and taken them out as a priority. And don't tell me you needed to go help Michael. We both know that as soon as that was all squared away you were back here looking for those damn crates, having us dig up most of the Chinese countryside."

"It was my—"

"Duty. No, it wasn't," Eve interrupted her. "And what about now? Is it your duty to be here babysitting our local space archeologist and helping him meet girls in cat-suits? No, it's not. You're avoiding. I've watched you. You've been all avoid-y ever since that perfect date you wouldn't talk about."

"Hey heyyyyy…" Giles turned around in his seat to get Yuko and Eve's attention. He was slurring his words, making Yuko suddenly wonder if he'd really been enhanced. "Listen to this," he said.

He ushered the girls over to sit at their table, pulling out the chairs across from Yuko and Eve. "Get this. These young ladies…"

One of them pawed at him like a cat.

"I, er, mean 'kittens,'" he corrected, "were telling me that our Empress doesn't have such a good reputation down here. Apparently, she's the stuff of nightmares—the thing that scares even the UnknownWorld."

More people in animal suits joined the cluster that had gathered around Giles as he spoke.

Giles looked at Yuko and Eve to see if they were as horrified as he was.

Yuko remained expressionless. Eve was still on the topic of Inspector Hirano, and was suffering from her conversational subroutine being so abruptly interrupted before she had accomplished her task.

"Anyway," he continued, taking another swig from his glass as two more guys swaggered up to hear what he was saying, "I was trying to explain that while she is quite the badass, she's actually quite the...well, *leader*. Formidable, yes, but that her people hate her and think she's a tyrant? I have never heard such a thing. Well, not until now."

He waved his now-empty glass at the kittens. "But it seems that a whole pseudo-religious movement has been gestating in her absence, like she is some matriarch of the planet to be feared. And the appearance of the ships…" His thoughts seemed to drift. "Well, it probably didn't help that image," he muttered to himself.

Yuko noticed the kittens were also a little bleary-eyed, which explained their tolerance for his conversation. However, behind their makeup and good manners they were sitting relatively still, perhaps pretending they weren't inebriated.

One of the guys muttered something about her being called a goddess from some legend.

"Absolutely!" Giles agreed, getting quite animated. "And she *is* a deity!" He stood up and raised an arm before he slumped butt-first back onto the chair.

He continued, "You should hear all the worlds she has destroyed, one after another. They whisper her name in even the fiercest of races, telling their warriors to beware. No one—and I mean *no one*—dares set a foot out of line where the Empress is concerned."

He paused.

Yuko looked up as two more guys in jeans wandered over with their drinks, as well as some guy in a suit.

And the dinosaur. Giles had gotten a *Gott Verdammt* dinosaur to come over to hear him speak, even sloshed.

Giles was oblivious at the moment, but it seemed like word of his insight into the happenings in the skies in the last few days had been getting around. He, however, was focused on the two silent kittens, who were gazing at him dumbly.

Eve had had enough of Giles' diatribe and turned to face Yuko, ignoring everyone else. "I'm your friend, and I want you to be happy. And that means pushing you to do the things you're scared of now and again."

Yuko put her hand on Eve's under the table. A tear had formed in her eye.

Eve urged, "I think you should go find him. He probably thinks you're going to just up and leave. You should at least have a conversation with him, and in my opinion, you should ask him to come with us, at the *least*."

Eve paused for a moment, then continued, "Of course

you'll probably need to get permission from Michael or Bethany Anne or someone, but given that their romance is the reason you stayed, I can't imagine for a second that they'd deny you your *own* chance at happiness."

Yuko felt the tear escape and drip down her cheek. Immediately she swiped it away, and amid the din of the music, the dry ice, the disorientating lasers, and the blacklight, she threw her arms around her friend and whispered, "Thank you."

Then she got up and left, somehow adeptly navigating her way past Giles as he poured himself another rice wine.

Eve watched her make her way through the crowd of gyrating animal bodies, but then she turned back and appeared suddenly between the cat-girls and Giles like an apparition with something important to tell the living.

"Giles," she said firmly, "I'm going to go now. Eve will see that you get back to the ship, but in my absence, there is to be no talk of our Empress at all. You hear me?"

Giles had started nodding to agree with her statement. Two seconds after she had asked if he heard her he realized he needed to do something different to indicate he had, so his nods turned to circles, mirrored by the movement of his glass in his hand.

"Good," Yuko confirmed. She shot Eve a glance that told her she had permission to enforce the decree and get him back safely, even if he turned into a handful. Eve nodded once, and Yuko disappeared again.

Giles looked over his shoulder, trying to see where she went, but after a second, he returned his attention to the kittens, who were still rapt.

He opened his mouth to speak again.

Eve glared at him warningly.

"Fine," he said. "Fine. *Fine. Fiiiinnnne.*"

He fell silent for a moment.

When he glanced up, even more people had joined their group. News of this strange man was spreading.

Giles smiled to everyone, raising an empty glass.

"Has anyone told you people," he asked, a large smirk on his face, "about Michael? The *Patriarch?*"

Out on the street, Eve moved the drunken Giles from a fireman's carry over her shoulder to the ground carefully so as not to break any of his bones. In the last one hundred and fifty years, the Empire had modified the nanocytes, reducing, in some cases, the all-or-nothing enhancement effort and propelling forward the medical capabilities of Bethany Anne's people. From what Eve could tell, he didn't have the right nano's to completely flush the sake from his system.

And there was probably a reason for it, given what she'd seen so far. It was rare for Bethany Anne to radically enhance a person until she was completely assured of their commitment.

Eve shook her head, wondering how best to deal with him.

"Oh my gaaaahhhd," he ranted excitedly from his horizontal position in the middle of the street, "this could totally be a new religion in the making!" He chuckled.

Unfazed by the fact that he'd just been carried out of

the bar for running his mouth, he continued his verbal stream of consciousness as he staggered to his feet.

With his legs spread apart to steady him, Giles blearily looked left, then right before he turned to Eve, whispering loudly enough that people a block away could probably hear him.

"Eve, imagine if we come back in fifty or even a hundred years for whatever reason and check in. I'll bet these people are going to be worshiping the goddess of the stars who came to save them, but also kicked ass and took names."

He gesticulated not just with his hands and arms, but with his whole body. He looked as if he were fighting an imaginary opponent.

Eve knew it was the sake.

And probably his youthful disposition.

Plus, the Shinjuku lights and atmosphere always seemed to have a strange effect on people.

Maybe she just needed to get him somewhere a little more...sober.

Yes, sober was good in all meanings of the word, she thought.

"Come on, Giles, let's get you back to the ship," she cajoled, like a grownup talking to a child.

Giles didn't respond. He was now seduced by the lights of the clubs around them. Eve grabbed his arm firmly and pointed Giles in the direction she wanted him to go.

He'd already caused quite a stir in the club, and she had been aware that people had followed them out. Calling a Pod in the middle of the club quarter probably wouldn't be the best idea right now.

Especially not after all his talk of gods and demons and...

Eve programmed the Pod to meet them on the outskirts of the quarter where it would be quieter. A few streets down the buildings were more commercial, and likely deserted at this hour.

She started walking with purpose, leaving Giles no choice but to keep up. "What? What's happening? Where're we going?" he asked, waving his hand over his shoulder. "But they were listening! I can't teach the truth of history or archeolothy...Wait," he looked up at the sky, "did I say 'archeology,' or 'archeolothy?'" He looked down at the little android, who was still walking determinedly forward.

Getting out of her grip was impossible. He had tried already.

Eve kept walking, her hand firmly gripping his arm. "We're leaving. The probability of this getting out of hand, causing a disturbance and affecting the perception of our operation has risen beyond acceptable parameters."

Giles stumbled along, trying to keep up with his arm.

He found his footing and muttered, "It seems you people down here are sensitive about your PR..." before surrendering to his fate.

CHAPTER TWENTY

Somewhere over the Northern Barren Lands of the Former USA

Giles' emotions shifted. He felt elated and desolate at the same time.

He'd read passages from spiritual texts which had suggested that extreme experiences could cause an "awakening." Maybe this was what they'd been talking about.

He guided the Pod over the continent that had been called "North America" in his father's time. His father, Frank Kurns, had talked about it now and again, generally when he was missing a particular whiskey the replicators couldn't simulate, but this was normally only after he had sampled two or three of the replicator's attempts.

He'd told of great cities buzzing with activity. Of staunch individualism. The urban jungles—concrete and asphalt, held up by an ideology that ran on the currency of debt.

He'd talked about the Chinese restaurant he'd lured

Giles' mother to, and of the something-or-other chicken dish which turned out to be their favorite.

How he would park a Pod many generations older than the one he flew now between towering buildings to try to avoid being detected by the authorities. They would have asked more questions than their operation at the time would have wanted to answer.

Giles had tried to picture this place and now, skimming the surface of this desolate wasteland, he found it hard to imagine.

True, in the more built-up areas Yuko had shown him around New York and the upper east coast of the continent it seemed plausible, but here? He sighed, feeling a deep compassion for the land he saw beneath him.

Spotting something up ahead, he slowed the Pod. The EI zoomed the cameras on what was below them. It was a gathering of people, but not a city. There were no buildings. Just tents, and…were those mats?

He zoomed in closer.

Yes, mats. People with their belongings next to the mats they sat on. And laid on.

He frowned, wondering if it was some kind of event, or party. But there was nothing else around except a stream about a mile away.

His heart crumpled in his chest.

These people *lived* like this.

"Maintain position," he muttered to the EI, trying to collect himself.

"Position held," the artificial voice answered. At times he wasn't sure if ArchAngel was running this for him or one of her subroutines, or he was flying the Pod himself.

Giles was stunned, and tried to absorb the scene as he steadied his breathing.

He watched a boy cleaning up some things and playing with a little girl on one of the mats. He had no shoes on. Well, neither of them did, but still, the little boy looked…*content.*

Giles became aware of tears running down his cheeks. He wiped his face, and then his eyes. "Goodness," he mumbled, chiding himself.

What became of our race?

His mind grappled with the abject poverty in front of him. Had he seen it in the archives he wouldn't have believed it, but here he was, not a stone's throw from his own people.

His brothers and sisters…suffering.

The cameras panned over more of the camp. Some occupants seemed to have tents and shelter.

"Computer, give me a climate evaluation for this area."

"Certainly. The climate in this area is relatively mild in terms of wind and rain. However, temperatures each night drop to freezing or below, and highs in the daytime reach extremes. Not ideal for human habitation."

"Not ideal at all," he muttered.

Giles vividly remembered a field trip to Zalifrax-2 he'd been dragged on way back when he'd first elected Archeology as his major.

There they were in cabins and the outside temperature would reach a chilly low—nothing compared to what these people were experiencing. But that had been one of the most uncomfortable experiences of his life, an experience that had made him pretty sure he wanted to study civilization from a distance, or at least from the comfort of a space station.

"Computer, land within five hundred yards of the perimeter."

"Acknowledged."

The Pod zoomed in and then hovered a foot above the sandy terrain.

Giles didn't know what he was going to do, but almost as if he were on autopilot he hit the button to open the door and got out.

The sand was hot—he could feel it even through his shoes—and the heat wafted through the air as well as reflecting off the sand.

He moved forward, barely able to walk because the sand offered little support for his steps.

The dryness in the air seemed to scorch the insides of his nostrils, and within seconds he started perspiring to deal with the conditions.

Every ounce of gray matter in his brain told him to get back into the Pod.

And yet...he *couldn't*.

He walked on, covering the stretch between the Pod and the camp.

People noticed him and started to gather at the edge of the mats. As he got closer he could hear them talking amongst themselves, wondering who this stranger was, coming out of a strange craft.

"Hi!" he said, shielding his eyes from the sun with his left arm and waving with the other.

The people chattered some more and the men pushed

their way in front of the women and children to protect what was theirs.

Giles held both his hands out, palms open. "I'm unarmed, and I'm not here to hurt you. I-I..." His voice caught in his throat and he ended up whispering the last words almost to himself.

"I want to *help*," he finished. He was embarrassed.

The leather-skinned men, their eyes creased from squinting in the sunlight day after day, regarded him carefully. One of them finally stepped forward. "What do you want from us?"

His hair had been blond once upon a time, but was now bleached white from the sun. The only indication of his age were his bright blue eyes.

Giles kept moving forward until he was a few paces out. "I was just passing through and saw your settlement from above. But...I wondered if I could be of assistance."

The man looked confused.

Giles kept talking. "I understand that the temperatures out here are extreme. Freezing or below at night..." his voice trailed off.

The man started to smile and said something to the men around him, who started chuckling and chattering amongst themselves.

"I'd like to help...if I can," Giles repeated.

"How can you help *us*?" the man asked. "You have a little...what's that now? A sky ship? And your clothes...you wouldn't survive out here come nightfall."

Giles glanced at his Pod, and then back to the man. "I..."

"Doesn't look like you're in a position to even help

yourself right now," the man observed, more confident now.

More people had gathered at the edge of the mats, and children pushed to see what was going on. Their faces were gaunt and drawn, showing signs of advanced starvation.

Those who were standing there curiously didn't seem miserable, though, and the children seemed...like children. Playful and happy, even.

Giles felt stupid for thinking he could help.

He took a step backward, the weight of ignorance heavy in his chest. *Stupid, stupid, stupid,* he cursed himself.

"I'm sorry," he called, putting his hand up as if to wave goodbye. "I-I was out of line. I'll go now." He stumbled and nearly fell over his own feet, struggling against the shifting sand.

He turned toward the Pod, feeling as if he had been mocked. How could he have been so naive?

His heart broke for these people, and yet he felt like an idiot compared to them. They were obviously dealing with their lives better than he ever could.

He started walking, biting back tears and trying to hold in all the emotion churning within him.

He wiped his face, nudging his glasses and then pushing them back into place. He thought he saw something out of the corner of his eye so he slowed and turned, looking again.

It was a child.

The same child he had been watching on the camera. He had left the crowd and was walking with him, trying to keep up as Giles headed back to his Pod.

Giles stopped and looked at the boy. "Hi."

The boy didn't speak, but he gave Giles a huge, toothy smile. He looked awkward, almost shy, but he wanted to communicate.

He waved his hand at the stranger.

Giles glanced back at the camp and saw that three or four other children had followed the first boy. They were laughing and waving…and smiling.

In that moment Giles couldn't keep back the tears anymore. His eyes started to leak uncontrollably.

"What's wrong, Mister?" the little boy asked.

Giles tried to answer.

The little boy grabbed Giles' hand. "It's ok. No matter what happens, it'll all be ok."

The other children caught up with them. One of the boys wrapped his arms around Giles' legs and hugged him and a little girl a bit bigger than the first boy put her arms up to be picked up.

Spontaneously—and still overwhelmed—Giles bent down and picked her up. Then he realized the children were cheering. Clapping. Laughing. The one who was hugging his legs was pulling at his pants to try to get him to come back to the camp.

The little girl whispered in his ear, "I think you should come back and talk to my dad."

Giles used the back of his other hand to wipe the tears from his face and started striding back to the camp.

"Seems the children want you to stay," the man with the sun-bleached hair called to him.

"Yes, er…it appears so," Giles agreed.

"Let me show you around. If you want to help us, you might as well see what we're up against."

Giles followed the man around the mats and through the camp, still carrying the little girl, with the entourage of children following in his wake.

"I'm Dwayne, by the way," the man with the leathery skin and young eyes told him, offering his hand as they scrambled over the sand.

Giles took it. "Giles."

Dwayne smirked amicably. "Sounds like a smart-person kind of name," he commented, leading the way across the sandy terrain.

Northern Barren Lands (former USA)

Giles was perspiring more than he ever had in his life, and the sun was burning the sensitive skin under his eyes and on his cheeks as it beat down and reflected off the sand.

The children were still following, but more quietly now. They knew not to overexert themselves in the middle of the day.

Dwayne waved his arms around as he explained the setup. "We're moving off in that direction now. Our scouts have found signs of water that way. If we can find water then we'll find food, and by this time next year we'll have a settlement and farms."

Giles shook his head in awe. "So you've been traveling like this for weeks already?"

Dwayne nodded. "Yes, ever since we ran out of water at the last place."

Giles pulled up his wrist computer and punched in some instructions to see if he could get a read on the distances involved. Dwayne watched in mild interest and one of the children poked his nose over Giles' arm to see what he was doing.

Giles frowned. "By my calculations you have at least another ten days of walking to get to anywhere that looks like it might have enough water."

He looked off to the north, trying to see any sign of anything but desert. He squinted, wondering if his eyes were playing tricks on him or if indeed there really were hills or something farther over that way. If there were hills, they'd get water. He knew enough of natural science and had done enough survival classes in hostile terrain (SCHT) to please his mother before his last field trip.

Dwayne scratched his head. "You're probably right," he agreed, looking back at the camp. "Many of them won't make it," he added more quietly so the children didn't hear.

Giles heard perfectly. His chest imploded, and the lump in his throat swelled. He tried to keep it together, since he'd feel like a fool if Dwayne saw him crying.

He coughed to try and hide his feelings and turned his back to think.

Eventually it came to him. "Let me take one of your scouts to the location you're interested in," he suggested. "In my Pod." He pointed at the ship he'd shown up in.

Dwayne had both hands on his hips. "How's that going to help?"

Giles shook his head. "Well, at least you'll know that's where you want to be, and that you're not heading to a mirage or a pipedream."

Dwayne shrugged.

"And if it is the right place, the least I can do is take a few people at a time—maybe the weakest—so they have half a chance."

Dwayne looked out at his camp. "There are over two hundred people here," he said, moved by Giles' kind offer.

Giles nodded. "I want to do everything I can. Let me start with making sure this new place has water."

Dwayne agreed and went back into the camp to find someone, while Giles and the chattering children headed back to his Pod. He answered questions about seeing an alien, and what space was like.

Dwayne met him at his Pod within ten minutes with a younger man. "This is Bernie," he said. Bernie had dark hair and darker skin, which wasn't quite as weathered as his leader's. "Bernie knows these parts, and he knows what we're looking for in terms of terrain and farm land."

"Good," Giles said, focused on his task now. He shook Bernie's hand. "Good to meet you, Bernie. I'm Giles. Shall we?" he said, waving to the Pod.

Bernie looked somewhat bewildered by the concept of stepping into a space machine with a strange person, but Dwayne clamped a strong hand across his shoulders. "We're all counting on you, boy. Do your thing, and hurry back."

The words mobilized Bernie, and Giles helped him into the Pod and the harness before stepping in himself.

Moments later the Pod silently took off and disappeared in the direction of the promised land, under the gaze of dozens of awestruck children and exhausted, dehydrated grownups.

· · ·

Northern Barren Lands (former USA)

Bernie hopped out of the Pod and immediately started exploring the new environment.

At first his senses were overwhelmed. There was rich soil beneath his feet, a certain sign of water.

Mountains were visible in the distance and there was gently sloping land all around.

There was moisture in the air, as well as the fresh scent of vegetation. It was if he'd stepped out of purgatory into a Utopian world of plenty.

He half-walked, half-ran a few paces, putting his hands into the shrubbery and inspecting the leaves as if he were an expert who had never seen such rich chlorophyll before.

Giles had barely managed to step out of the Pod before Bernie was off, finding his way through a break in the shrubs and trees toward the sound of water.

Bernie hadn't gone many paces before he realized that they were in a valley, with a river just ahead and flat plains beyond.

"This is perfect for farming!" he called back.

Giles hurried after him. Panting, he caught up, joining Bernie in a small clearing.

"Yes, this'll do. This'll do quite nicely," Bernie said, a slight twang in his voice as well as a note of relief. He seemed refreshed.

The air here was cooler. Milder, almost even gentle on the skin. Giles grinned. "Ok, then, back to camp," Giles instructed, marching back toward the Pod.

Bernie started to follow, but paused. "Why don't I just wait here?"

Giles stopped and shook his head. "Nope. First you have to let them know that this is where you recommend, then I'll bring you back."

"Ok…" Bernie agreed slowly, not quite understanding why they should waste a trip.

Giles nodded and started walking again. There wasn't time or reason to explain his understanding of human behavior when said humans were fighting for survival.

They needed reassurance from one of their own. They needed to know that he hadn't harmed Bernie. They needed to trust him if he was going to get as many of them over here as he could.

Bernie, unfazed, followed Giles back into the Pod and strapped on the harness as Giles had shown him.

As the Pod door closed, Giles hailed the EI. "Computer, track our course. I'd like to automate the flight between here and the camp so I don't need to be present."

"Tracking," the artificial voice responded, making Bernie nearly jump out of his skin.

Giles grinned. "Alien tech," he said, nodding. He felt very satisfied, as if he'd waited his whole life to deliver those two words.

Bernie broke into his first smile, a smile which in a heartbeat turned into a chuckle. By the time they were speeding back to the camp, it had turned into a full belly-laugh.

When they got back to the camp, Bernie jumped excitedly down from the Pod after a minor false start where he'd forgotten to undo his safety harness and half strangled himself in the process.

He ran across the sand to the others as a crowd started to gather again. Dwayne appeared and Giles watched from the Pod as the two men talked. Bernie pointed at the Pod and then in the direction of the new land.

Dwayne nodded. His eyes held the genuine concern of a leader carrying the weight of responsibility.

He knew he needed to take this leap of faith and trust this stranger who had dropped from the sky. There was no other way of saving his people.

Even so, he wasn't blind to the consequences if the stranger wasn't trustworthy.

He just had to hope and pray that the genuineness and compassion he had seen in the stranger's eyes was the real deal.

He called for some of the other men and sent them toward Giles and his Pod, then he followed.

He greeted Giles with a handshake and a big smile. "Looks like we're in business!"

"It does," Giles agreed. "You'll have yourself a wonderfully pleasant new home very soon."

Giles started explaining. "I've programmed the Pod so I don't have to go each time. You can probably fit two adults, three if you push it, and add in a few of the little ones," he said, smiling at the kids who had reappeared around him and were striving for his attention. The little girl from before put up her arms to be picked up and he obliged, feeling slightly out of place in the child care department but touched by the innocent affection nonetheless.

Dwayne smiled as he watched Giles as he held the child and put his hand firmly on Giles' free shoulder. He had a tear in his eye. "Thank you," he said quietly.

The two men shared a moment of complete understanding. Not as one man doing something for the other, but as an exchange. As two human beings being able to fulfill for each other what they had been struggling to do alone.

To contribute. To make a difference. To change the fate, the suffering, of their brothers and sisters.

Giles started to tear up too before quickly turning to talk gruffly of the strategy for the moving operation, and how to determine who should be transported first.

Minutes later the Pod took two men and one of the children off to the new land. Their task was to set up a few water stations and maybe even some shelter before nightfall.

Dwayne left to start organizing the rest of the camp and get them to form an orderly line. This was going to take a while.

QBS *ArchAngel II*, Bridge, Orbiting Earth

"Yes," Akio admitted, "I can acquire Terry Henry's location easily."

"Let's do it." Bethany Anne sighed. "There are so many relationships involved in making this happen, and so much sadness at times that it is hard for me to be around." She called to someone to her left before turning back to Akio and Michael. "We will get those in Japan first."

"Change is hard," Michael admitted from the seat to her right, and when she turned to him he continued, "It is what it is. We need to acclimate everyone to the ships and to what their future will be if they come with us. We can't stay too long on Earth. We'll run into the same set of petty squabbles the old government tried to press on TQB before."

"They can try," Bethany Anne retorted.

"That is my point," Michael agreed. "They have neither the emotional strings to pull anymore, nor the financial or military strings. You are not willing to play diplomat at all, therefore your armada is attractive to them. The longer we are here, the harder they will try to manipulate friends and family—good people—to get a toe-hold, and what then? We lose a ship by destroying it with all hands aboard?"

Bethany Anne sighed. "Humans," she said, looking toward the screens showing Earth beneath them, "are insidious, manipulative bastards who are fantastic at worming their way into getting what they want."

Why do you think I believe I got lucky? TOM asked her. **It's the same spirit you have, except you care for others. Michael is right. The longer we stay, the higher the chance someone somewhere is going to get lucky. You will be forced to retaliate, and that will be on your conscience for a thousand years.**

If I make it that long. She huffed in annoyance. "Ok, let's get our people, make sure we have finished all the tasks we have to do, and get the fuck off this planet. We aren't helping it by being here."

"Nope, we aren't," Michael agreed.

Bethany Anne stood up. "We are going to need the *War Axe* to retrieve our people in Japan."

As they left Akio asked innocently, "I was introduced to someone Terry Henry would like to meet. Anyone seen Dokken?" he asked. "I understand he was also helped in the Pod-Doc a while back?"

His voice, wafting down the hallway, became very serious. "Michael-san, you *have* to be introduced to Dokken, I assure you our trip to Earth will not be complete without the experience."

Michael's grunt of acceptance confirmed to those who heard them that Michael didn't expect it to be a pleasant experience.

CHAPTER TWENTY-ONE

Northern Barren Lands (former USA)

Dwayne wandered over to Giles, who was once again standing at the edge of the camp looking off into the distance.

Dwayne handed him a cup of what he told him was coffee. It wasn't coffee as Giles knew it, but it was a kind gesture and he accepted it gratefully.

"This is going to take a while longer," Dwayne said, glancing back at the encampment. It still seemed just as populated as it had been hours before when they had sent the first Pod-load off. "Maybe we'll be going all night."

Giles sipped at the coffee, then nodded as he swallowed. "Maybe," he agreed, "but it will take as long as it takes."

The sun was starting to go down, so the heat wasn't as uncomfortable as it had been, but the sweat on his skin was turning cold and making him long for a hot shower.

"Aren't your people going to be worried about you?" Dwayne asked, a hint of concern in his voice.

"Me?" Giles snorted a small chuckle. "Nah. Probably haven't even noticed I'm gone."

There was a pause.

"Oh yeah?" Dwayne said, waving his coffee mug to Giles' right. "I wouldn't be so sure." Dwayne looked into the distance, so Giles did too.

There were four Pods in the sky above the horizon in the fading light, making their way across the desert land.

"Well, I'll be…" Giles whispered under his breath.

Dwayne grinned, a kind of wholesome, faith-restored-in-humanity kind of grin.

Giles' comm tingled on his wrist, almost causing him to spill his coffee. He opened the channel.

John Grimes' voice boomed unceremoniously through his audio implant. "Heard someone was mounting a rescue mission without us!"

"Mr. Grimes!" Giles grinned, all reverence evaporating in an instant as he switched into jock-mode. "How did you find me?" He felt stupid for asking the question as soon as it left his mouth.

He heard John and the other Bitches laughing heartily. He blushed and glanced sheepishly at Dwayne, who looked pleased as punch that reinforcements had shown up.

John cut in over the laughter, "You have been tracked the whole time. ArchAngel allowed you your space after Yuko and Eve put you to bed. Once she put your rescue mission on the satellite monitors, Bethany Anne sent us out to help."

"Oh, excellent," Giles responded. "So you brought a few extra Pods. Great!"

Giles' slight sarcasm wasn't lost on the Bitches, and they jeered at him.

Then Giles realized why.

A second later a large ship appeared behind the Pods, turning on its search beams and illuminating the ground beneath it.

It made the Pods disappear.

"Didn't think we'd do half the job, did you?" John chuckled.

Giles felt foolish, but laughed despite himself. "Touché, Mr. Grimes, Touché."

The people behind them seemed fearful, but when Dwayne shouted to them to tell them what was happening their fears turned into cheers.

People started getting up from their mats and packing their belongings, hugging each other and crying and laughing and celebrating.

Dwayne was hugging his team and spontaneously threw his arms around Giles, pulling him into a group hug and knocking his glasses askew.

As Giles reached up to reset his glasses, the faces of the people in the camp were burned indelibly in his brain.

It was a moment Giles would never forget, not in his whole long life.

Northern Barren Lands (former USA)

Barnabas stood on the tail ramp of the *G'laxix Sphaea* watching the last of the refugees board.

Eric and Scott were inside helping them get settled and

distributing water bottles they'd picked up from somewhere on the way.

Darryl had set up a temporary Sickbay to treat those who had injuries or extreme dehydration.

He found himself setting up drips, although he'd never done one before. For the last forty minutes he'd been telling people that he wasn't an actual doctor when they thanked him and called him "doctor," but after drip number twenty he just gave up and said, "You're welcome."

He even overheard one of the younger girls who'd been brought to him by her sister giggle and call him "Doctor Gorgeous" when his back was turned.

"Well, I guess that's the last of them," Barnabas reported to Eric, striding up the tail ramp to take a shortcut through the crowd in the holding bay rather than walking around to the side door via the sand.

Walking on sand when one didn't have to was a silly thing to do.

Too inefficient.

Dwayne and Giles followed the last of the people onto the ship, and Giles hit the comm at the side of the door. "Hello, Captain? We're all on board now."

"Acknowledged," Kael-ven replied. "Closing now."

Giles and Dwayne watched the artificially lit desert disappear as the ramp came up and enveloped them in comforting technology.

Dwayne turned to Giles. "You know, I really cannot thank you enough. I mean, if you hadn't come along, who knows how many of us would have made it?"

Giles nodded. "You know, I think somehow the fates made it so." He pulled up a map on his wrist computer and showed it to Dwayne. "Coz this was the direction you were heading," he pointed, "and this is where your new home is." He pointed again, moving the map several inches to bring their new destination into view.

Dwayne's mouth dropped open. "You mean we weren't even going in the right direction?"

Giles shook his head and put his finger to his lips. "And this was much farther. Much better this way," he said, smiling.

Dwayne shook his head in disbelief as he looked around at those he thought would have been dead in a few days. "I'm a terrible leader. These people would have died."

"No," Giles said firmly. "You're an excellent leader. You gave them hope and purpose. The technology you had let you down. And sometimes we can do all the right things and still not succeed, which I think is the point of what I'm trying to tell you. You are an excellent leader to these people. They look up to you. They trust you. You are going to face challenges along the way, and no matter what doesn't go according to your plan, I want to leave you with one thing: You. Are. An. Excellent. Leader."

Dwayne was having difficulty processing everything.

Giles needed to ensure he would remember the point he was making. "Sometimes we're doing all the right things, but still things don't go our way. Instead of judging your success as a leader by what goes your way, judge yourself by the process. Can you take people with you? Can you inspire them to be the best version of themselves? If the answer is yes and everything else goes to shit, then you've still done your job, in my book."

Giles looked at the people milling about and laughing.

Some of the kids had started throwing water at each other, and the adults were laughing at their exuberance.

"Look at it this way," Giles told Dwayne. "Without you they wouldn't be so happy. Without you they would have turned on each other long before you had even left the settlement. Because of you, they have a chance at a new life. A new home. This," he said emphatically, "is your legacy, and your people need you."

He slapped him on the back and left the leader to his own thoughts, disappearing into the crowd to enjoy the celebration of a few hundred lives saved.

The people stayed on the ship that night, and when the sun came up the Bitches and some of the support personnel they had brought with them helped make sure the new settlement had a few shelters built and access to water.

By midday Barnabas had started pulling in the troops, ready to leave.

Giles had been helping build shelters and was reluctant to leave, but after saying some fond farewells he made his way back to the ship.

The Pods had already disappeared, including his original one.

The *G'laxix Sphaea* had warmed itself up and the ramp was six inches from being closed, so Giles scrambled quickly to one of the side doors.

Only to find it locked.

He hailed Barnabas on the flight deck. "Hey, Barnabas,

wanna let me on board?" he asked, trying to keep the concern out of his voice.

The ship started to lift off…*without him.*

"Hey, guys? *Guys!*" Giles smacked the side of the ship before it rose too high to reach.

He put his hands beside his mouth. *"GUYS!"* he shouted at the top of his lungs.

Dwayne and his team had stopped what they were doing and were bent over laughing. They pointed up at the window of the flight deck.

Giles walked backward to see what they were pointing at. John, Darryl, Eric, and Scott were up there laughing hysterically as Giles panicked, thinking he was going to be left in a new colony.

"Thought you might like another field trip." Grimes chuckled into his ear piece.

Giles, flushed and exasperated and almost ready to have a heart attack, finally let go and laughed at himself.

He stepped backward one more time, made several choice gestures at the Bitches at the window, and then fell backward on the ground in surrender.

The ship stopped lifting and came back down. When the door opened Barnabas was standing there with a look of pity on his face. He helped Giles scramble onto the ship before closing the door and signaling for takeoff.

"Sorry, Giles. I told them not to, but you know them. They're a little wired with all this do-gooding."

He had a faint smile on his lips. "As soon as I realized what they were doing I put a stop to it. Well," he pursed his lips, thinking about his earlier talk with Giles, "relatively soon after." He looked at Giles, "You're good?" he asked, putting a kind hand on his shoulder and walking farther into the ship. "You're good!" he told both himself and Giles.

Giles was exhausted and scared half to death. The raging emotions had him looking for a quiet lounge area and something to drink.

He barely got to the door of the lounge when the four guys caught up with him.

In cheers and back-slaps they teased him and then congratulated him on a job well done. Within minutes he'd had a beer shoved into his hand and was being treated like one of them.

Like a brother.

John pulled him aside for a moment and explained quietly and simply, "You're one of us now."

Giles pointed at John and then the others. "One of the Bitches?"

John chuckles, shaking his head. "No. I don't think you want that kind of ass-kicking all of the time. However!" He put up a finger. "I'm happy to call you one of the team." John jerked a thumb over his shoulder. "You did good out there. You stepped up to help those people, and you didn't flip out when we gave you shit. You're good, Giles." He slapped him on the back and then sat down with the others, leaving Giles dazed and overwhelmed.

But for once not feeling like an outcast.

QBS *ArchAngel II*, Orbiting Earth

The next morning, still awash with mixed emotions about his adventure, Giles settled into one of the smaller meeting rooms he'd commandeered for his books and study.

He'd spent much of the morning researching, which actually meant staring vacantly at the wall between multiple cups of coffee.

He was *compos mentis* enough to ensure that he at least sat with his back to the door so no one would see how unproductive he was being if they happened to walk past.

This afternoon he'd been a little more productive in the thirty minutes he'd been actively applying himself. Having found nothing specific in the most likely books, he had managed to find some general references to certain artifacts that had been found in prominent places.

Mostly in various tombs across the Loop galaxy. Plus he'd found a few crackpot theories in the archives which suggested that this unphotographed artifact may have originated someplace as yet unexplored by the Empire.

He sighed and sat back in his chair, his mind wandering to the events of the previous day. It seemed almost surreal to be back aboard the ship with all the creature comforts: caffeinated nectar, hot showers, and ionized air conditioning.

Somewhere in his subconscious he was aware of high-heeled boots striding down the corridor, although his conscious mind was far too distracted to pay attention to the sound. He leaned forward, grabbed his coffee mug, and brought the soothingly hot liquid halfway to his lips.

BANG! BANG!

Someone knocked on the door and he turned, cup in hand, to see the Empress herself looking at him.

He nearly jumped out of his skin.

"Knock, knock," she said, granting herself access to his hideaway. "Mind if I come in?"

It was clearly a statement rather than a question, because she was halfway through the door before he found his voice.

"Er, yes. I mean...of course," he stuttered, slopping his hot coffee on his lap and then setting the cup down, trying not to yelp or make a big deal of the molten liquid scalding his groin and splashing on the open book in front of him.

"Heard about what you did yesterday," Bethany Anne said. "Good job."

Giles' eyes nearly popped out of his head and he started to choke with shock at the comment, and indeed the *compliment*, from her Highness.

"You ok?" she asked, a smile creeping across her lips.

She knows goddamn well the effect she has on people, especially boys. Men, he corrected himself firmly.

He finished coughing. "Erm, yes. And thank you." He awkwardly pushed his glasses back up.

Bethany Anne glanced around the room, clearly amused. She perched herself on the table inches from where he'd set down his coffee mug.

Giles reckoned that if he were to reach for the handle right this moment he would probably end up brushing his hand against her thigh.

And that would be a very, very baaaaad move, he decided quickly. Not that he was thinking of doing it. It was just... It felt like one of those random, compulsive thoughts, like seeing a car wreck in one's mind and hoping it would never happen.

Not that he wouldn't, you know, love to... *Just. Stop. THINKING*! he scolded himself.

He glanced back up at her to see a certain amusement in her eyes. That was when he realized…

SHIT. She's reading my motherfucking mind!

Her eyes rested on the stacks of books on the table and those scattered in front of him. "So what are these for?" she asked, tilting her head.

"Well, they're research," he said, not being able to resist smiling despite feeling like a goon.

"Which you dragged onto my ship, taking up extra weight, and have to transfer to your next ship."

"Right."

"Giles, why the *fuck* do you carry books?"

Giles played along and pretended to look confused. "Well, er, they have information in them."

She shook her head. "Academics and books." She sighed. "They come as a package, like hipsters and conde-scension."

She moved toward the door, causing a flood of relief through the young space archeologist's system.

"Oh…" She turned back. "Just one more thing."

"Uh huh?"

"The talisman you...separated...from the rest of the Sacred Clan boxes. Make sure you tell my dad about it, understand?"

Giles spluttered, "Yes. I mean, yes. Yes, of course."

Her eyes flashed red and Giles thought he was going to wet himself. He pushed his chair back again, terrified, his hands up in front of him. "I swear. Of course I will! I was just—"

"Researching it, I know," she said simply, her eyes back to normal. "You might also want to mention to him that you'll need an upgrade. Can't have you doing your archae-ological-civilization-saving thing and falling prey to malaria or whatever shit goes on out there." She paused a moment. "Or advanced amounts of alcohol."

She'd already turned her back and was almost out of the room. "And remember next time that you have a team and comm for a reason. *Use* them."

And with that she left, the sounds of her high heels moving down the hall signaling her departure.

Giles exhaled and then sat depleted in his chair, as if he hadn't already been a wreck before Bethany Anne's visit.

When his world stopped spinning he realized that not only did he need to pee badly and he'd been holding his breath, but also that his skin was covered with sweat.

He glanced at the slopped coffee and dozens of disheveled books. "Holy fuckwipes of a Yollin's pancreas," he muttered under his breath.

That should be creative enough for her.

He slowly got to his feet. *Restroom, then water, then shower...*

And then if he was still in shock, he fully intended to check himself into Sickbay.

Her words were still ringing in his ears: "Your archaeo-logical-civilization-saving thing." He filed it away for later, too confused for it to sink in.

He wandered out of the room with the back of his right hand to his forehead, hoping he didn't die of stress before he managed to get an upgrade. Otherwise his academic biography was going to be very, very short.

CHAPTER TWENTY-TWO

Outside Earth's Atmosphere

Bethany Anne's ambassadorial ship, little more than a luxury shuttle, departed the *ArchAngel II* followed by a squadron of fighters flying cover for the Queen as Bethany Anne, Akio, and Michael transferred to a Defender-series destroyer.

They needed the heavy-lifting capabilities the *War Axe* could provide if they were to free the trapped Queen's Elites in Japan.

As soon as the shuttle entered the landing bay, the destroyer pointed its nose toward the planet and headed into the upper atmosphere. It skipped and bounced during its steep descent as it streamed fire.

The captain had discussed the best way to inform those on the planet that the Etherians had had enough of some of the bullshit that had been tossed at Bethany Anne's people in the last few days.

Half the world saw the harbinger flaming through the sky.

The *War Axe* raced through Earth's sky at a speed in excess of Mach 30.

The ship slowed and dropped off Akio's Pod as it worked its way around the main island of Japan, making sure everyone saw the might of the ship.

The *War Axe* approached the Pod hovering a half-mile above the collapsed building Akio had protected for the past hundred and fifty years.

Eight stories under some hundred-thousand tons of rubble, six Elite warriors awakened from the deep sleep which had helped slow their aging. They had been buried inadvertently back when chaos ruled the world.

The time right after the WWDE, and Akio could not have saved them without risking their lives.

So he had waited. With infinite patience, Akio, Yuko, and Eve protected both their world and their team to keep the world from destroying itself.

They had *almost* failed.

But Akio had found help. Former Marine Terry Henry Walton and his werewolf partner-wife Charumati had joined forces with the Queen's Bitch to drag humanity back to civilization, a hundred and fifty-plus-year effort.

The *War Axe* descended, slowing as the gravitic engines surged to control the bulk of the ship. Akio directed the ship to the building, and then his Pod moved back.

The Defender-series destroyer had the Etheric Empire's latest traction to tractor-beam technology. Using all the power available to it, the ship latched onto the building and picked it up en masse.

The beam held the rubble of the destroyed building

together as the ship slid sideways and dumped it into a clear area beyond.

The Japanese government had already given permission, otherwise it might have taken a bit longer. Yuko, the Diplomat, had told them in no uncertain terms that this would be happening, and that any effort to stop it would be deemed an act of war.

You didn't attack a mercy mission.

Akio's Pod, a small and boxy ship to shuttle troops and equipment from planet-side to orbit, swooped above the hole and stopped in mid-air, then dropped. A hundred feet down the Pod settled, and the rear ramp dropped.

Six vampires were waiting. Their clothes were old, largely just rags after more than a hundred and fifty years.

Akio stepped out and bowed deeply to his fellows.

"It has been too long," he told them.

"*Hai!*" one of them said with a big smile. They hurried silently and anxiously onto the shuttle, as if a delay would condemn them to be buried anew.

Akio acknowledged that everyone was on board and the shuttle lifted gracefully out of the hole and headed toward the mighty ship above.

Bethany Anne was waiting.

San Francisco, Western Shore, Old United States

Terry Henry Walton, TH to his friends, stood tall and proud, his black Force de Guerre uniform crisp. His were-wolf wife Charumati watched him, her eyes sparkling purple in the morning sun. His people were anxious, excited, and afraid. None of them knew what to expect, and they all had different ideas.

A massive and fantastic vessel approached from the west—from Japan—just like Akio had told him it would.

TH caught Char's wince out of the corner of his eye. He reached for her hand and looked adoringly into her purple eyes, as he often did, and asked, "What's wrong?"

"So many from the UnknownWorld feeding off the power of the Etheric," she replied, crows-feet appearing around her eyes as she fought the pain.

Joseph and his wife Petricia stayed close to Terry, as he'd asked them to do. It was his turn to protect them; payback for all the times they'd had his back. Joseph and Petricia were Forsaken, but they were different. They refused to drink human blood.

Terry Henry and these two Forsaken had fought side by side. TH considered them his friends, and would stand by them during the introductions to make sure nothing went wrong.

To the best of his ability and beyond for his family and his friends.

Joseph had joined Char's pack well over a century earlier. As the werewolf pack's Alpha, she had vouched for the Forsaken as she'd vouched for the weretigers in the pack.

It wasn't a normal pack, but nothing about TH and Char's life could have been considered normal anymore. Terry Henry had worked with Bethany Anne in the far distant past, but would be a minor blip at best in her memories.

He wasn't sure she would recognize him or remember

the stray moment in time their paths had crossed. How important would that time be, which had happened here on Earth, compared to the rest of her experiences in the universe beyond?

Terry Henry considered who was on that ship.

Bethany Anne and Michael, the universe's answer to justice. For Bethany Anne, it was simple. She hated bullies, and seven of the Kurtherian clans were comprised of bullies. When they collided with Bethany Anne, the very stars shuddered at the impact.

The Kurtherians of the Seven she had encountered had lost, because humanity would not be denied and mankind's champion *refused* to lose. The love of her life would be waiting for her, Bethany Anne believed, but first she had to survive and return to Earth.

And now she was back.

She was back with Michael by her side, and the universe breathed a sigh of relief.

The *War Axe* descended slowly, regally. They had cleared the transshipment area of the wharf for the ship to land, but had underestimated the vast proportions of such a vessel.

"This ship is not that big compared to the *ArchAngel*," Terry said excitedly to no one in particular. Next to him, Char clenched her jaw as she struggled with the energy flows of those aboard the ship.

Terry looked at the assembled group of his friends and family and nodded.

Most didn't notice.

Marcie winced and gasped. Marcie had been gifted

nanocytes from her mother, Felicity, who was one of the enhanced.

Felicity was nearby, holding the hand of her werewolf husband, torn between watching the ship and comforting her daughter. She chose the latter, moving close and draping a protective arm over Marcie's shoulder.

Felicity and Marcie were both raving beauties with blonde hair, blue eyes, and lithe bodies. Felicity was a socialite, but Marcie had chosen a different path. She had found her niche. She was a warrior's warrior, the deadliest of the deadly.

Terry and Char's adopted daughter Kimber put a hand on her brother Kae's arm. The family had always been close. More than a century had passed, but time didn't matter.

Family did.

Charumati's pack was there as well. Standing farther away from the ship, and well away from the vampires.

Sue, Timmons, Shonna, and Merrit shuffled impatiently. The mated werewolf pairs fought for their alpha and their friends.

The weretigers, Aaron and Yanmei, were relaxed in the company of the werewolves. The pack had been together for a long time. It had been exactly one hundred years since Yanmei joined.

Ripples across the Etheric were hitting the most sensitive of them like waves hitting a beach.

A lower hatch on the ship opened and a stairway unfolded to the pavement. All eyes were on the ship, and the person who started to walk out.

CHAPTER TWENTY-THREE

Akio was the first person to step out.

Terry exhaled heavily. He hadn't realized he'd been holding his breath. Char released his hand and wiped the sweat on her pants.

She moved closer and wrapped her arm around Terry's waist, and he kissed the side of her head. When he looked back at the Pod, Akio had been joined by six other vampires.

Char recoiled as they approached. Terry had guessed that they were the Queen's Elites who had been trapped when an earthquake dropped a building on them during WWDE.

Now he was sure.

Akio stopped, and the Elites fanned out behind him. Akio bowed deeply to the Colonel and his lady—more deeply than he ever had before.

Terry and Char returned the bow at a perfect ninety-degree angle, and their children, who were ranged behind them, did the same.

Akio stood up straight before approaching and shaking hands with Terry and Char, a smile on his face and a glint of humor in his eyes.

Was that a real glint of humor, TH wondered, *or was he seeing things?*

Akio waved to the people standing with the Colonel.

A group left the Pod, strolling casually toward TH and Char. The Elites stepped aside, creating a corridor through which they could pass.

A dark-haired beauty walked at the side of a man who wore a long black coat and a black hat.

His eyes took in everything while remaining focused on Terry Henry.

They stopped before passing the last of their vampire escorts. The woman's eyes flashed red as she glanced from one face to the next, lingering on Joseph's.

TH stepped forward, which drew the attention of the Elites. Their hands seized pistol grips and sword hilts, but he held his hands up.

The man chuckled silently and the woman smiled crookedly, practically rolling her eyes at all the posturing before she focused on the man in front of her.

"We've met before, Empress," Terry Henry said. He dropped to one knee and bowed his head before continuing. "I'm sorry. Akio asked us to help him prepare this world for your return, but I failed him. I failed *you.*"

Char stepped forward and put a hand on her husband's back.

Her eyes glistened. This was supposed to be a joyous return, but TH, as he always did, took responsibility for everything—whether in his control or not.

Empress? TOM asked.

I'll deal with telling everyone I've gone back to "Queen" some other time. It always becomes a long-assed discussion on the Federation and my proclivity to recoil from that title. That's how they know me for now. I'll switch it later.

Bethany Anne shook her head. "Cut the 'Empress' bullshit, Terry. I remember you from the Antarctica operation."

She raised her voice to make sure everyone heard her as she tapped a finger to her lips. "You were hypothermic, if I remember correctly, before we put you in the Pod-doc."

She looked around before continuing, "My name is Bethany Anne, and I'd like to introduce Michael." She glanced past everyone, taking in the sights and sounds of San Francisco. "Things look pretty damn good from where I'm standing, TH." She turned to the purple-eyed woman next to TH and winked. "And you must be Char."

Bethany Anne held out her hand, with no hint of subterfuge. She stage-whispered, the humor obvious in her face, *"Trust me, behind every strong man is a strong woman."*

There was a snort behind Bethany Anne, who caught the slight glint of amusement in Char's eyes from Michael's unspoken retort.

Bethany Anne rolled her eyes. "Oh for fuck's sake, stand up, TH! You're making me feel weird."

"Listen up, people," she said, projecting her voice for those without enhanced hearing.

She rolled her eyes. "Would you *stop* imitating a police academy cadet review?" She gestured them forward. "Come up here, and let's talk like folks who have kicked some ass and now are going to get a little well-deserved R and R."

The group hesitated, but Char too waved them over. Felicity dragged Ted toward the front of the mob. When she looked at the Queen's feet she stopped abruptly, grinning.

She pointed. "I just love those boots!" Felicity exclaimed in her southern drawl.

Bethany Anne aimed a finger over her shoulder at the man behind her to prevent the comment she just knew Michael was straining to keep in as she replied, "I know, right? Finally, a woman with taste!"

She finally turned to Michael. "See? It's all about the shoes."

"San Francisco has some of the best shopping in the world if you can spare a few hours," Felicity added.

Bethany Anne looked up at Michael. He struggled mightily, jaws working as he grimaced, but finally he surrendered and let his eyes roll.

"And Michael will go too," Bethany Anne said. "I've been away from this hunk of mostly hairless hot stuff for way too long."

Michael pursed his lips and commented, "It's growing. It's just taking a while."

She looked at the group who now formed a semicircle around her. "I wanted to meet you personally and thank you for everything you've done, both in my name and on your own to help make the world a better place. Akio said he could not have chosen better—even if he'd had a choice."

There was a rumble of laughter at that and she paused a moment before continuing, "What we've found across the universe is that no matter how hard we try, we can never fully defeat evil."

She shrugged. "It can be stomped into the ground." Bethany Anne put up her fingers, just an inch apart. "It can be sliced into little fucking pieces, but where one is removed, another takes its place. Fucking cockroaches! We can relegate them to the dark places, the slime and swamps in which they breed, but they'll always be there.

"No matter. You have helped make the world safe for humanity once again. You have carved a chunk out of life's cesspool, and you have handed it over so those who remain can make their own way. Self-determination and all that."

She sighed as she took them all in. "And now you have some choices, one of which is to take the rest you deserve. God *knows* you deserve it, and it's yours if that is what you want."

She smiled for a moment. "However…" She paused and winked at Terry Henry. "You knew there was going to be a 'however,' right?"

Bethany Anne got the chuckles she was looking for as she waved a hand at the massive ship above them. "I want to invite you to take the *War Axe* through the Annex Gate and join my father, Lance Reynolds, in securing and expanding the brand new Etheric Federation."

She smiled mischievously. "There is a little side business called 'the Bad Company' I think you and your people would be *perfect* to slide right into." She looked at TH and Char. "What do you think about exporting your brand of justice to the whole fucking *universe?*"

Bethany Anne didn't wait for an answer before continuing.

She pointed up, but her focus was strictly on the man in front of her.

A man who had walked through his own version of hell, the guilt over what did and *didn't* happen during the WWDE. It had taken TH decades to come to terms with his responsibilities when he chose to come out of the mountains twenty years after WWDE and change the lives of those around him.

One day at a time.

Bethany Anne continued, "The sky beckons warriors, so come home to your place, TH. Earth will survive without you, because you have taught it to. You've done your duty. Your legacy will live on here, but I have a *new* mission for those willing to step up. To take your skills and your get-shit-done attitude to a place that will cause your eyes to pop.

"Come home to the stars. Come home to the Etheric Federation." She looked at the group. *"All of you."*

Terry squeezed Char's hand, and they smiled at each other. He looked at the rest of the eager faces. It was everything he never knew he wanted. He opened his mouth to speak, but...

Before he could answer, a huge German Shepherd-looking dog vaulted from the ship, raced in a wide arc around the Elites, and slid to a stop near Terry and Char, wagging its tail furiously as he looked up at him.

Like he had found a new toy...Or maybe a friend.

"Who's a good boy?" Terry said, wearing a ridiculous grin as he took in the dog. Char tried to keep her face calm as she watched her husband, who just couldn't stop himself.

Michael answered from behind Bethany Anne.

"He knows who the good boy is. This is Dokken, Terry Henry, and he's pretty smart. When and if you get a chip in your head, you'll be able to communicate with him."

Michael turned to the panting creature, who was staring up at him. "Yes? Are you sure? Okay, have it your way." Michael shrugged and turned back to TH. "Dokken says to tell you that he thinks you're a good boy too."

Terry started to laugh in the way a person does when he's among friends.

CHAPTER TWENTY-FOUR

QBS *ArchAngel II*, Heading Toward New York City State

"Because," ArchAngel, the AI of the ship, told Bethany Anne, "you are too valuable to be out there with only Michael. John and the others got into a barfight in this very city."

"A barfight?" Bethany Anne asked her own face. "You want to go down and help Michael pick up Valerie because of a *barfight?*"

"They have flying ships, so there is danger." She sniffed.

Bethany Anne's eyes narrowed. "Wait a minute…" She pointed to the screen. "You want to show off! This is from the reports of the *War Axe,* isn't it!"

ArchAngel hesitated before answering, "I am a digital sentient being. I do not need to show off."

Bethany Anne's eyes narrowed. "When do you believe the best time would be to accomplish this?"

There was no telltale hesitation of an AI calculating the answer—ArchAngel already had the answer ready. "In the evening. The weather pattern shows that a cloud bank will be present from which we can descend at the same time the rays from the sun setting in the west highlight the ship."

"Uh huh." Bethany Anne waved a hand. "Set it up with Michael. I'm joining him to pick up Valerie and whoever wishes to come." Bethany Anne pointed a finger at her ship's avatar. "But don't be scaring the locals…"

She finished her sentence as she headed off the bridge, "too much."

Those in New York City State were very aware of the humans who had returned. Their efforts around the world had been recorded, and when possible, the recordings had been sent to those in power.

To both proper power—the authorities—and to improper power, the criminals.

On the top of the fifteen-story Jackson Building, which had been renamed after Conner Jackson, a man who had died in a recent battle to protect the city, a couple were dining quietly. By candlelight, even.

Not that they needed it to see, for there was plenty of light from the advertisements above them, and the waning light of sunset still glowed in the west. There were no other buildings close, so there were lots of floating vehicles heading back and forth above them and below them.

They ignored the cars.

The woman had blond hair and a medium tan. She chewed her food, but then used her fork to punctuate her comments as she and the other spoke. "I'm telling you, it *is* possible to take out one of their ships." She swallowed as she leaned over the small table. "Bobby, we could use that ship to help us acquire a few more, and then decide if we can run up enough to take over one of the bigger ships."

"Are you *daft,* Chelsea?" he asked. His mouth was open, his food-laden fork forgotten. "Do you have an ounce of logic in your brain, or is it *completely* full of stupid?"

"See?" She glanced at him, her eyes agates as she cut her meat. She stabbed it with her fork, but then used it to point at him. "You lack vision!" She stuck it in her mouth, continuing to talk, "You have the spine of an earthworm wallowing in the mud. You need me," she swallowed, "to point out the possibilities." She looked back down at her food. "And you can call me 'Barbara Anne' from now on."

"Whaaaaa*AAAT*?" Bobby sat there a moment, his hands on the table. "You're changing your name now, too?" He shook his head, "And her name is 'Bethany Anne,' not 'Barbara Anne.'"

The woman rubbed her nose. "I'm aware of that." She corrected her posture. "But I don't want to change my hair."

Bobby looked at his partner in crime, thinking of the reckless ideas she had put into his head over the years and how many times he had accomplished those stupid things so she would admire him.

Now he recognized exactly what he was to her.

A pawn. A patsy. Someone she was using to climb the ladder. If he failed, she would jump on the next man and suck *him* dry, until he was used up or had provided enough for her sense of self-worth. She was still talking, her fork waving, but he tuned her out.

The stupidity of her latest idea had finally allowed him to see through to the dank core of her heart. He sighed, put down his fork and knife, folded his hands over his belly, and leaned back, enjoying the evening air.

For a criminal he wasn't bad. He didn't hurt others on purpose, and those Chelsea had encouraged him to destroy were in his profession too. One day he rather expected to be gunned down by someone like him.

Perhaps someone else with their own Chelsea driving them to accomplish great things for their own ego. But this Chelsea?

It was at that moment the massive *thrum* caught his attention. He leaned over to look down the street, where a lot of the air vehicles were turning, making sharp rights or lefts to get out of the flight lanes or going below the approved in-city flying altitude.

The cars on the ground had all stopped, and people were getting out and pointing behind him.

Bobby turned to his left, ignoring Chelsea, who was getting annoyed because he wasn't paying attention. He ground out, "You need to pay attention too, you stupid bitch."

His lips pressed together as she started calling him names.

In front of him a large ship, black in color, was slowly moving between the buildings. Now this was a vessel! Its majestic presence took his breath away as it slowly floated down the street at the same height as the roof of his building. The white logo of a female vampire with fangs fairly stared at him as it went by.

Something touched his mind as he watched the ship pass, then a male voice spoke to him.

Rabid dogs always come to an end, and how many people do they kill before it happens?

As the ship passed, Chelsea stood across the table pointing to it. "That one!" she exclaimed as she watched it. "That's the one we will start with." She turned to face Bobby, excitement in her eyes…until she noticed his gun pointing at her head.

He shook his head. "No, *we* won't."

"What are you doing?" She stomped her foot, her lips sneering. "Don't be a boot-licking spineless—"

A bit of her brain splattered the roof's deck but some went over, no doubt dropping to the street below as her body jerked backward and hit the safety wall before slumping to the floor. Her eyes were open, but lifeless.

Bobby slid the gun back into its holster as one of his men turned to call inside. Bobby picked up the napkin and wiped his mouth before he stepped around the table and squatted next to the lifeless woman. "I'd tell you it was the gods talking to me who told me to kill you."

He reached forward and closed her eyes, "But the truth is, you were a heartless bitch who already ended too many lives, using me as the weapon. I couldn't let you go, because there would have constantly been guys gunning for me with you pushing them from behind." He stood up, nodding to his men, who had brought a large canvas tarp. "Sometimes the tool gains wisdom."

He turned his back on her and walked away, heading into his suite.

Bethany Anne was in her suite watching the video Shinigami had taken of the incident. "Did Michael cause that?"

"I believe Michael played a part," Shinigami answered. Her face was in the corner of the video. "He was in the front of the ship searching the minds of the people around, looking for Valerie."

"We could always just announce ourselves."

"True," Shinigami replied in that tone that said, "Only if you make us."

Ten minutes later, Michael sent word that he had found Valerie and was going to take the silver shuttle down.

Bethany Anne acknowledged his message and agreed she would meet him back on the *ArchAngel,* which was hovering behind them.

Allowing Michael a moment to greet his protege without her around.

A shadow fell over the city. At first Valerie thought it was simply another storm, but then a familiar voice called, "Valerie, I hope this isn't a bad time."

Valerie, her friend Sandra, Sandra's husband and their baby named after Valerie, and finally her partner-in-crime Robin turned to see Michael walking toward them on one of the broad streets of New York.

Above him a silver shuttle hovered, and past that a

spaceship larger than anything Valerie had ever seen took up most of the sky to the east.

It had to be several times as large as the whole city of New York!

"My...Dark Messiah," she greeted him, bowing her head. "Is it time?"

He smiled and nodded. "Terry-Henry Walton is already aboard and looks forward to seeing you again. He brought a friend, so I will extend the offer to you to do so as well." His eyes moved past her and he nodded. "Welcome, Robin."

Valerie had almost forgotten that he could read minds, so she blushed.

"Thank you."

He nodded. "Please say your farewells, and let's be off. We have a war to win. We want to leave the area so Bethany Anne does not have to respond to attacks." A small, grim smile graced his face. "She has become less patient even than I when she is responding to provocation. I might have to work on that with her."

Michael smiled a half-second later. "Imagine that, if you can. I am to be the person who encourages restraint!"

With that he turned and the shuttle dropped into the center of Capital Square. People left a wide space around it and watched in amazement, many heads turning from the advanced shuttle up to the sky and back down once more.

A few spoke of gods and goddesses, and Michael tried to keep his eyes from flashing in irritation. There was nothing he could do except ignore the comments.

He moved forward and a door opened for him, and he stepped up into the shuttle. They could just make him out as he sat there waiting. At first Valerie hadn't been sure it was him since his head wasn't completely bald like it had been when they had first met. As they approached, though, there was no doubt.

"So this is actually it," Sandra said, careful with the baby as she gave Valerie a one-armed hug. "Fuck! I mean," she covered the baby's ears and blushed, "I'm going to miss you. I really will. I'll write you, let you know how we're doing. Is there a way to get letters to you?"

"I'll ask," Valerie promised. She hugged Diego too and then turned to the shuttle, her eyes moving with awe to the large ship above. "I have a feeling this is going to blow my mind."

"You and me both," Robin replied.

You two have no idea, Michael's voice said in their minds, and they looked at each other with wide eyes.

"Here we go," Valerie said.

"Into the great beyond to kick alien ass," Robin agreed.

"Let's make it count."

Together they gave Sandra, Diego, and baby Valerie a final wave, and walked forward to enter the shuttle and begin the next stage of their journey.

CHAPTER TWENTY-FIVE

Nagoya, Japan, Hirano Residence

Yuko touched down in her Pod outside Hirano's residence, then sat for a moment watching the breeze blow a blossom across the parking lot.

She knew she had to face him, but her mind churned with all the possibilities of how this might go. What if he wasn't interested anymore? What if he had a girlfriend now, or worse? What if...

What if?

She stopped herself, realizing that she was just working herself into a state. She glanced up at the windows, trying to figure out which was his. Eve had already done a scan and confirmed by the location of his handset that he was home, so all she had to do was walk up to the door and see if he'd buzz her in.

Her heart felt like it was going to explode. She hit the button to open the Pod door and stepped out into the breeze, bracing herself against the slight difference in temperature.

In a moment she had crossed the asphalt to the entry and rung the button as if it hadn't been any time at all since she was last here.

"Hello?" Hirano's voice came through the intercom.

"Er...hello. It's me. Yuko." She paused, waiting for his reaction.

There was a long silence.

"Ah, er... Hello!" He didn't sound displeased to hear her, but he certainly wasn't jumping for joy. Her heart sank, and every second of silence crushed it deeper and deeper in on itself.

She wasn't sure what else to say. Her mind started scrambling for ways to explain why she was back, and why now and not before.

But no words came.

After what seemed like an eternity, though, the buzzer sounded. She moved to push the door open while she had the chance and slipped inside.

The walk from the front door to his apartment was the longest distance she'd ever covered. Every step gave her new pause for thought.

It took all her training and will power to keep pressing forward. She knew she was walking toward disappointment and rejection.

She arrived at the door, which was slightly ajar, so she pushed it open and stepped inside. The place looked the same as it had the last time she had been here, although it was maybe a little tidier. She wondered idly if she had caught him the day after his cleaner had been there.

"I'll be there in a second," he called.

Yuko waited just inside the door. Sunshine streamed

through the windows as if the outside world didn't know or care that her world was about to end.

There were shuffling and scrambling sounds in what must have been his bedroom. She wondered briefly if there was someone in there with him.

Eventually he appeared, his hair freshly combed and damp as if he were fresh from the shower. He wore a button-down shirt and a casual pair of slacks. If Yuko didn't know any better she would have guessed that he had in fact just showered and dressed.

"Hi," he said brightly, standing in the doorway.

"Hi," she parroted. "So I..." He started speaking at the same time, so she waved for him to go ahead and he did the same.

She lowered her eyes. "I wanted to see you before we go."

He looked disappointed. "So you're leaving?"

She nodded, a hand gesturing toward the window. "It's my duty. My life is out there...with my people."

He leaned against the doorframe, his eyes on the ground. "So you just came to say good-bye."

"Yes." she answered, but then a small voice which sounded suspiciously like Eve's added, "Well, no. It depends."

He glanced up, confused.

She straightened her shoulders, "It's like... Well, I made a mistake, Hirano." She moved her hair out of her eyes, "I wanted to keep you safe, but that wasn't a mistake. And I needed to go, but it wasn't that recently. I mean...I'm not explaining this very well."

She took a deep breath and tried again, this time using

her hands as she rambled. "I realized over the last few weeks that I'd been using that as an excuse. I was scared that the people coming after us were going to kill you, but I was also scared of...*us*. And now we're leaving in a few hours and it's the last chance I have to see you and I wanted to ask... Do you want to come with us? I mean, with *me* specifically?"

Hirano had a smile in his eyes as he looked up, but despite all her skills in reading body language she still couldn't tell if he was really pleased or not.

Anxiety washed through her. His answer was either going to be very, very bad or very, very good—there was no in-between at this point. She held her breath, waiting.

"I'm glad you came to talk to me," he started slowly.

Yuko felt from that his tone was about to let her down, and he was just being polite.

"But…" he continued.

She nodded. It was a polite let-down. He was probably involved with someone else and didn't want to leave his life here. Or he was committed to the job. She didn't need to know the details. She sighed, trying desperately to hide her disappointment.

She started to leave.

"But I wish you'd come to see me sooner. I've been waiting all this time with no way of contacting you."

Yuko turned back around. "You mean you still feel the same way?"

For once the Diplomat had nothing in her arsenal that allowed her to understand. Her own emotions were doing to her what countless others had tried and failed to accomplish.

They confused her.

Hirano grinned as tears welled in his eyes. "Yuko, of course I do. I just wish you hadn't left me hanging all this time."

He didn't move.

She narrowed her eyes. "You mean you were just…"

"Keeping you hanging so you had a taste of your own medicine?" He chuckled. "Pretty much," he confessed, still not budging from the other side of the room.

Yuko couldn't decide if she wanted to kick his ass or kiss him, but in an instant, she had crossed the living room to him and he had lifted her up in a hug so tight that she thought he'd perhaps found some nanocytes of his own.

He spun her around, kissing her face and any area of her he could contact with his lips.

Yuko sat at the kitchen bar watching Hirano make tea. "You know you can bring some things with you!" she told him.

Hirano shrugged and checked his handheld. "I'm just waiting for my friend Zen to call me back. I'll leave the apartment and everything to him. He has friends... Cousins, even, who could use it."

Yuko twisted around to look at the place. "You'd walk away from all this just for me?"

Hirano grinned and peered at her from under his eyebrows. "And for adventures in space," he teased.

She giggled and leaned her arms on the countertop.

He looked around too. "I need to pack some clothes to wear, but everything else is just stuff."

Yuko nodded. Having spent a hundred and fifty years on Earth, she had come to the same conclusion. It wasn't that she didn't appreciate all the things she had and had built, but when push came to shove there were things that were far more important.

Like friendship.

Like loyalty.

Like *love*.

She smiled, content to watch Hirano putter around the kitchen.

His handset started to ring and he answered it. "*Hai. Hai,* Zen. It's happening. She came for me."

Yuko sat up straight. He'd been planning this. She glared at him playfully as she put it together. He glanced over and winked at her.

She made a show of putting her hands on her hips and scowling, and he started laughing before he headed out of the kitchen into the living room so he could pay better attention to the conversation with his friend.

Yuko listened. She didn't mean to eavesdrop exactly, but she wanted to know exactly what they said and her vamp hearing afforded her the luxury without too much effort.

"Yes. I want you to have that too. I'll leave it in the safe. You can use it to tell the stories to your grandkids," Hirano told Zen.

She could hear Zen laughing on the other end of the line. It was a bittersweet laugh. Apparently they'd had numerous conversations on the topic. It also seemed that

Zen was thrilled for his friend's good fortune in finding the love of his life and having a chance to be with her.

But he would miss him dearly.

The two men ended with quiet words of respect and wished each other the best of fortune in the years to come.

"I'll never forget you, Zen," Hirano said softly.

"Nor I you, my friend," Zen replied before they hung up.

Yuko's heart was heavy, and when Hirano stepped back into the kitchen she had tears streaking her face. "I feel awful, pulling you away from your life."

He wrapped his arms around her. "I am blessed to have some good friends, but the one thing I've learned so far in my very short life is that the only constant is change. I'm excited to move on to the next chapter."

Yuko could feel his heart beat as he held her. She could tell he was crying, but despite that he seemed ready.

"We should pack up and go," she told him. "The ships will be leaving, and we don't want to miss our ride."

When he released her, though they both had tears they were smiling, their eyes full of hope.

"Ok, I'll go pack," he said, squeezing her shoulders before he hurried off.

Yuko knew Bethany Anne would not leave her behind, but she didn't wish to have the Queen Bitch herself show up and tell her she would put her size sevens up her ass if she didn't get a move on.

She smiled, knowing she was home.

Home wasn't a place, like this apartment or the ships above. It was who you were with, and how you worked it out together. She had stayed with her parents on Earth waiting for Michael to come back, and her Queen and her family had come back for him and for her, Akio, and Eve, Terry Henry, Valerie, and the others.

And her family had grown larger by one person this day.

She whispered, knowing full well that somewhere on her body was a bug her sister had planted on her. "I love you too, Eve."

Hirano came out of his room with two suitcases. She reached for one of the suitcases and he held them back, then smiled and handed one to her, which gave him the chance to hold her around the waist as they each carried a suitcase into the next stage of their lives.

Somewhere in the world dawn had arrived. Not just physically, but in her heart as well.

QBS *ArchAngel II*, Orbiting Planet Devon, Bethany Anne's Shuttle Bay

"You can't bullshit a bullshitter," John told Kiel as he, Akio, Eric, Michael, Darryl, and Scott waited for Bethany Anne to hitch a ride down to Devon, the planet she owned.

They had finally left Earth, some ships heading back toward the fledgling Etheric Federation and some ships coming here, to the planet she had been working to hide for the past few years.

Kiel shook his head. "No, no bullshit. I'm here to retire, maybe have a female for longer than three months." He shrugged his shoulders. "Harass Kael-ven."

"Ha!" Eric pointed to Kiel. "That's what brought you here…Kael-ven!"

Kiel shrugged. "I decided on the *G'laxix Sphaea,* that much is true."

"Kael-ven's staying?" Darryl asked, "I mean, once we go out again?"

Kiel nodded. "I think we are both ready to live a sedately dangerous life."

"'Sedately dangerous?'" Michael asked, "I'm not sure I understand that phrase."

Scott answered. "Devon needs to be straightened out, so a few of us who will be living here will," he raised his hands to apply air quotes, "'occasionally,'" he dropped his hands, "help stomp out shit that is going on. It's a rough planet, and we are mighty, but we are few."

Kiel flipped his right hand to one side, then the other. "Plus, I still get to play with armor and high-velocity firearms."

The men chuckled. Michael turned a moment before everyone else when Bethany Anne had entered the shuttle bay. "Be back, guys," he told them and walked toward her.

"Something different about the boss?" Darryl asked.

Scott said, "You mean, other than getting some?" *POP!* Scott looked at John and rubbed his shoulder, "Ouch, you bastard! What the hell?"

"Super-hearing?" John said, pointing to his ears.

"I am not *that* base," Scott answered, "but I appreciate the warning anyway."

He started walking in her direction with a look of confusion on his face, and Bethany Anne slowed down and waited for him to join her. "What's wrong?" she asked, not sure what Michael's look meant.

"You are different," he explained, moving a bit of her hair over her ear.

She swatted at his hand. "Stop that!" She grimaced when some of the hair fell back into her face. She tried blowing it back and looked at Michael, who was smiling at her problem. She pushed her hair back again and pointed at it. "Your fault!"

He smiled. "I got what I wanted," he told her. Then he stepped a little closer and his eyes locked on hers as he looked into her soul. "What. Is. Different?" he asked, his breath warming her.

"Michael, I just want to say this wasn't planned." She looked up, but he was already starting to put two and two together.

"I'm pregnant," she told him.

His eyes shot open. "YES!" he shouted. He grabbed her under her arms, lifted her off the ground, and twirled her around.

Bethany Anne was laughing. "Put me down. I'm not a blender here!" she argued, but he ignored her for a moment, her feet flapping as he spun her around and around. The two of them laughed in concert.

Michael gently slowed down, bringing her in for a kiss as her feet softly touched the deck.

"So," Bethany Anne played with his shirt. "Along with our dog…"

"And cat," Michael added.

"Daughter Tabitha," Bethany Anne said.

He nodded. "Wards Mark and Jacqueline, and other daughter Eve."

"Ah, Eve." Bethany Anne nodded.

"Six Bitches," Michael continued. "Although we need to add one so I can inform them we have changed their names to the Seven Dwarfs."

"I'm sure John will be pleased." Bethany Anne nodded. "And a fleet of people and ships."

"And a planet to run."

"And another planet to keep hidden and safe…"

"We will now have our own child," Michael whispered. There was a tear at the corner of his eye. "I'm going to be a *father*."

"You already are." Bethany Anne raised up on her toes and kissed him. "We are just adding one more very special child."

He pulled her closer. "Thank you, Bethany Anne. When I met you I was training my replacement, ready to walk into the sun."

She smirked, a hint of humor in her voice. "I *sent* you into the sun, remember?"

He chuckled. "Yes, and please do me the favor of never doing that again—like ever. I can't come back from that."

She hugged him hard. "I won't ever let you go, Michael Nacht."

Because I'm not raising this child alone, you bastard, she added, mentally.

I heard that, Michael replied.

Good.

This knowing what you are thinking is going to make for a very interesting life, Bethany Anne.

Damned right it will.

You have to have the last word, don't you? he asked, humor coloring his mental speech.

There was a long pause before she replied.

No.

He chuckled, leaving the discussion where it was. Together they turned toward the guys and walked over, ready to go down to the planet they would call home for a while.

Then they would continue the search for the Kurtherians.

Together.

FINIS

First, like I have done sooooo many books before, let me THANK YOU for not only reading through these stories, but reading these author notes, as well!

Ok, full disclosure – This was both the hardest book to write, and the easiest. The hardest because I had to go back, and connect various scenes from Life Goes On (TKG21), Gateway to the Universe (Craig Martelle and Justin Sloan) and Return of Victory (Justin Sloan) all into this manuscript while I connected with Ell Leigh Clarke on the parts she wrote.

I was DREADING that aspect (the connections part.) So, I worked to integrate with Ellie's on her parts. That was relatively easy because she was so far ahead of me, that by the time I had fifteen thousand words left, she was just about done (or was complete I think.)

<<Ellie Edit: I'm always the easiest part of any equation :D. Ooops. Hang on… Delete! Delete! Delete! >>

So, I get her manuscript, merge it into my manuscript and change all the fonts so that it looks the same to me.

I think I only had one major goof-up that I found before I got the order of all of the scenes corrected. I read through the whole document (leaving those big sections I mention above until the end.)

Then, I downloaded the books I thought I would need (failing to download Gateway because I didn't realize I didn't already own the book.) I went through the books on the flight back from London to Las Vegas and marked up the stories.

That was Monday.

By Monday night, I had a plan to work for the quick Boris scene and shot it to Paul C. Middleton for review, and I thought "I've got this!"

By Wednesday afternoon, I had both this book, and Life Goes On to the editing teams, and my mind just started to flounder.

<< Ellie Edit: I'm already confused…>>

I had been working on one or the other of these two books since Christmas. Now, they were done!

About that Physics Question…

On Thursday or Friday, I was looking at my phone, playing with the Facebook app and I saw a conversation I remembered (then) that I had during my flight from Las Vegas to London (I think I was in London Heathrow maybe at this time?). A fan had asked a *very* scientific question, and there was no way I was going to be able to answer this without a keyboard.

At least, not easily.

So, I texted them that I would need to get back to my

laptop to answer their question, and slid the phone back into my pocket.

Where I promptly forgot that I needed to answer the question until I got back home to the US. Actually, I think it was a couple of days PAST that time.

So, I'm at home, looking at my phone again and open that same Facebook application. This time, I see the question again (mind you, I'm still on the phone) and re-read their question.

"Huh," I think. "This is a physics type question. I'd bet Ellie (Ell Leigh Clarke) would be a better person to truly answer this question, and I'd look smart for getting her involved."

So, the next day or so, Ellie happens to mention that "she answered the fan."

I thought this was *FANTABULOUS*! It took me a while before my mental processes slowed down enough, that my eyebrows started to narrow together as I questioned, "How?"

You see, I hadn't actually gotten around to sending her the question for the fan. I mean, I'm cool if the fan reached out to her without me getting involved, just surprised.

Upon further discussion, it's obvious the reason that Ellie was able to answer this question was because "I" didn't realize that when I saw the question, I was actually in the Admin section of HER Facebook page.

Fortunately, I wasn't in Zoom (or Skype) at this time, or she would have seen how red my face had been. That section of the FB page I feel is for her personal messages to fans, and I pride myself on staying the hell out of that area.

<< Ellie Edit:… mostly. But he says that like a guy who

prides himself on never checking his gf's phone… only to be caught red handed two days later. Yup. This happened to me. Years ago now… but this just reminds me of it. (And not that I was even bothered at the time. More just amused). It's the nobility… that comes before a fuck up. Tee hee hee :P >>

Not *ONLY* had I gone into that area, but I didn't realize WHERE I was when I was talking to the fan… as *Ellie*. Telling the fan that the BEST person to answer the fan's question *WAS ELLIE*. How much more confusing could I have *POSSIBLY* made it for the fan?

"Hello fan, I know you asked the question to Ellie. But apparently, Ellie is going to answer you (not explaining it's actually Michael answering) and tell you to ask Ellie…"

Which they had already done.

Ellie tells me a moment later that she had done a kick-ass job of answering the question.

Here are the messages that truly go with this story:

BT (fan): Okay, I've had some questions for a while and you seem like just the author to answer them. Specifically, can/does a dimension exist like the etheric? Even if it's just a mathematical representation? How would it be possible for someone to cross dimensions? Wouldn't the energy required to bridge dimensions make any energy transference far to inefficient to be useful for powering weapons? And kind of a related question from recent SciFi, would a particle accelerator really be capable of "ripping space time" and causing dimensional collisions? What would even happen if two dimensions collided? Sorry if it's too many questions or you don't want to answer them but you seem to be the science knowledge behind the series so I thought you'd have some of the answers.

<Note how they never specified "Ellie" and I just assumed they meant me?>

From Me (replying as Ellie): hey BT, I need to be at computer to respond to these. Lemme come back to you soon! :)

BT: Absolutely I look forward to learning and discussing.

Now, 1 week later (Thursday to Thursday):

Thursday at 1:24PM I reply: So, I've been in England since you asked these questions- some I think Ell Leigh Clarke and MD Cooper would know more, some I can guess at.

I mention Ell since she is a physicist.

Are you curious for a reason or to scratch an inquisition itch?

Now, thank goodness, Ellie realizes my FU and jumps on to HER messages, and answers BT who must be scratching his head at this point:

Ellie (6 hours later): Hey this looks like MA has jumped onto this msg thread... so this is Ellie again... When I came on board and started playing with the etheric, MA and I talked about how it ties up with the physics. I decided, and MA kinda went along with my sciency back story, that this could be a vector space known as the Calabi-Yaw manifold, which is a versatile 6 dimensional space which is used in things like string theory and quantum loop gravity to make the maths work.

Re the energy - yes it would... but more than that, stretching space time in that way right now is nigh on impossible. Anything that exists at that scale (plank scale) kinda bubbles in and out of existence. Then, if we look at concepts like black holes and worm holes (i had a whole rant about this with MDC on a podcast episode we recorded) nothing can survive even part of the black hole journey - let alone anything else.

Re the particle accelerator... yes, the smashing action can cause us to view some of these plank scale phenomenon - but only in terms of the particles it throws off. Conceivably this could cause a slight rippling, though I don't think we have tech to detect it. I'm sure there are some equations somewhere that try to model that - but you'd have to be using a gravitation wave model of the standard model i think (modeling particles as waves).

Re dimensional collisions, just look into any brane theory stuff. I think there is a great review paper on M theory that talks about applying brane theory (modeling universes) as branes and the effects of that: the big bang, new universes, lots of consecutive big bangs etc etc . Basically though, no one knows the answers to these questions, but we can hypothesize about what might be, and then make mathematical models to fit the ideas... which then spur more ideas and "understanding". Hope this helps! It's a lot to answer in a msg... :)

BT: Yes. It is a lot to answer for sure. I wish I could say I had a practical reason for asking but the honest truth is I'm just curious. And you seemed like the physicist to answer the question. It's surprisingly hard to Google and find coherent answers to questions like interdimensional energy transference. I guess the last question I have if you're willing to answer (aka isn't a plot point I've missed).

Why would someone be able to transfer between dimensions yet have an entire dimension (etheric) be unobtainable/surprising when accessed?

Thank you so much for your detailed answer!

Now, Ellie answers with what I knew to be true (but I had rather she had stayed with the aforementioned cool answers.)

Ellie: Ah you're talking about BA and Michael? That's just coz the author decided that was the physical set up of their universe. That's all :)

After this, our fan comes back with:

BT: Actually Molly. She is able to travel through dimensions yet when she accesses and is able to fee BA the general and Adam both seem concerned that she's able to access that dimension.

And, in true Ellie fashion...she punts to the future. (Right where I wish I could have put the answer!)

Ellie: AAh yes.. that's all still unfolding.

Now, this is how the story unfolded on our SLACK channel:

Ellie: Hey, was this you? (She provides a screenshot of the previous message (the one I told you about up above.)

Then, before I can answer, she says:

Ellie: ps. i just answered him. I'm such a badass. (eyeroll)

Me: Yes, that was me... I was reading on my phone, so I didn't realize I wasn't on my personal channel.

sorry! :-/

And you are a badass.

Ellie: yeah, but you're saying that without even looking at what i wrote him! :-o

Me: True, but that's because I am ashamed that I was

answering your questions in the first place. (I consider it 'yours' - so, I don't go in there...).

Do you want me to check?

Ellie: No. Don't bother. It's just geeky shit. Nothing interesting ;)

Now, I go to sleep, and I don't remember if I saw this before I went to sleep, or at something like 4:30AM in the morning, when I wake up.

Mike (4:35 AM): Grrrrr, now I will HAVE to ... :-)

Mike (5:12 AM): Holy crap!

Can I grab that?

Damn, now *THAT* was an answer!

And that is the story of how you get a physicist to answer a fan question!

... by getting involved in their own messages and mucking everything up!

Thank you SO MUCH for reading these stories, and I look forward to seeing you again when the next series with Bethany Anne, Michael, Akio, Yuko, Eve, Mark and Jacqueline start up: The Kurtherian Endgame!

Ad Aeternitatem,
Michael Anderle

AUTHOR NOTES - ELL LEIGH CLARKE
FEBRUARY 11TH, 2018

Thank yous

MA

Big thanks must first go out to my collaborator, Mr. Anderle.

As you know this tickles me that I get to have my name *under* yours… (Snigger, snigger). Yeah, some of us just have a dirty mind. Dear reader, you may have to re-read that to see where I was going with it.

It also amuses me that you (MA/ yoda/ the boss) have to do the final punch for a change. Hahahahahahahaha-haha. Seriously though… thank you for having me on this project and trusting me with your baby.

It's been a blast! Truly – thank you.

Steve and the JITers

Thank you also to Steve Campbell and his team of JITers.

Steve is aka. The Silver Fox, according to my friends in the UK who saw our picture on fb recently...! He didn't protest it, so it's kinda stuck. It's how I introduce him to anyone now :)

<Steve Edit: Silver Fox = Old Guy. And, just so you know, it's awesome having the last word on these author notes :)>

Apart from allowing me to give him a new nick name every book, he also smooths the process of editing, proofing and publishing so that I can be completely hands off. Steve, you're a life saver.

Our fabulous Just in Time team are awesome too. In reading and proofing the final product before it goes to the Zon, you give us peace of mind. Knowing that we're not going to get slated for bad punctuation, typos, gaps in the stories, or even downright blatant inconsistencies, is a huge help.

You've also been super awesome in helping me fact check stuff when I'm in the grind of writing and just can't recall certain details that whole scenes will hinge on. You're the best, and I'm forever grateful for your input and support. Thank you!

Amazon Reviewers

As always massive thanks goes out to our hoard of Zon reviewers. It's because of you that we get to do this full time. Without your five star reviews and thoughtful words on the Zon we simply wouldn't have enough folks reading these space shenanigans to be able to write full time.

You are the reason these stories exist and you have no idea how frikkin' grateful I am to you.

Thank you, from the bottom of my heart.

Readers and FB page supporters

Last, and certainly by no means least, I'd like to thank you for reading this book… and all the others. Your enthusiasm for the world, and the characters, is heart-warming. Your words of encouragement, and demands for the next episode, are the things that often stay in my mind as I flick from checking the facebook page to the scrivener file when I start each writing session.

It used to be that caffeine was my drug of choice.

Now it's you.

Thank you for being here, for reading, for reviewing, and for always brightening my day with your words of support on the fb page. You rock my world, and without you, there really would be no reason to write these stories.

Thank you <3

Ellie and Speed Reading

Since starting this indie publishing game I've been talking about how I should learn to frikkin' speed read. Then maybe I'd have a chance of… I dunno, reading my collaborator's previous books so I'd get shit right.

Or maybe just even be able to re-read something that we're meant to be working on the sequel for… and being able to recall what we wrote the first-time round.

The reality has been that as we work on more and more series (Michael, Molly, Giles…) it's becoming increasingly difficult, and important, to have it fresh in one's mind. And this problem is only going to get compounded as we fire up new series in this universe, and the Ellie'verse. (More on the Ellie'verse in a moment.)

So finally, after a certain fan mentioned his reading speed on the fb page - and MA made another comment about how I'm *still* behind on reading his 21-book-master-pieces - I got my act together and googled "speed reading courses".

Within 15 minutes I was signed up to a big ass course that is going to teach me how to be a "Super Learner."

Rather than just increasing my reading speed, it's also promises to help me remember what I read!

Perfect.

So far I'm only a little way into it, but I can feel my memory improving. About 3/5 of the course is all about memory techniques.

Not only that but I've been coming to the awareness that when I've been struggling to write it's not so much that I'm "mentally burnt out", although that's been part of it. But more than that, I think my brain has been bored.

Yup.

Believe it or not, it's not been getting the right kind of stimulation.

So where I was using ear plugs and orange glasses just to try and cut out the "noise" the bigger problem seems to be I just wasn't giving it new information. I haven't been taking in non-fiction in the way I always used to. Plus, I'm coming off a three-year book hiatus because when I was nomadic I couldn't carry them. (I'd even given my kindle away because I didn't want the luggage weight. I will rethink this differently in future, mark my words!)

Plus I'd been so busy DOING that I "didn't have time".

Well, as I'm getting more and more into this speed reading/ memory thing I'm finding my hunger for learning has been returning. I've been buying physical books again. (Man, I love paper!) As well as reading stuff on the Kindle that MA bought me to try and get me to finish reading his series!

It's been working.

My daily word count is up, I'm recovering my physical strength and focus, and everything is on the up and up.

Woot :D

I think moving to Austin is working for me too…

Plus practicing presence and surrender has been a big turning point. But in terms of getting (coherent!) words on the page, having a constant input has been awesome.

Anyhoo – for those who are interested, my reading speed at the beginning of the course was about 255 words per min.

This is *abysmally* slow.

Slower than average. Honestly, I dunno how I survived this long.

The guy who is teaching the course reads 1500 words per minute with an 80% retention rate. I can barely believe that is possible, but he's the one I'm shooting to emulate. Even if I get half way to that it will change my life.

But with this new-found hope, I've actually been

starting to read faster I think… though I haven't measured it again yet. I noticed how it wasn't that painful to read Michael 3 in preparation for writing this book – Michael 4.

MA also noticed I knocked it off over the weekend… rather than it taking me 8 weeks to get through it.

I think something is working.

Reading Michael 3 (Darkest Before the Dawn)

Clearly I needed to catch up on this because I couldn't remember all the threads and details that we had to incorporate into the next episode.

But I kinda also needed to know what had happened on the Michael/ Akio side of the adventure too…

Confession: I had no idea until I read it a few weeks ago. I mean sure, we had discussed beats… but MA doesn't seem to stick solidly to what he said he was gonna write.

PLUS, a lot of stuff evolves as one writes, so the published version was essentially a whole new story to me.

Even the bits *I'd* written…

I'd be a few pages into a scene and be like:

hmmm, this feels familiar.

Oh shit, yeah, I remember writing this.

Yup. I know. I'm slow. But hey…

It reminds me of a game I played once in primary school.

You know, the one where you send a note around in class and every adds one line to the story? And you end up with a completely bizarre off the wall tale.

Well reading back through M3 was kinda like that.

Now that this series is complete I can now confess that I didn't read MAs half at all during the process.

I know. Shoddy work on my part. But on the flip side, I *totally* trusted my awesome collaborator to stitch it together in the way that only he knows how.

And thankfully from the reviews for M3, it seemed to work.

Let's hope it did for M4!

Michael 4 was a little trickier though as there was a lot more going on.

Not only had MA cleverly woven BA 21 together with it from Michael's perspective, but we also had a tonne of stuff to pick up from Michael 3: like Hirano, who if we left behind we would never be forgiven by you guys, like the baddies that needed killing, and like the Sabine-Akio thing that needed clarifying.

Sabine and Akio

So I'm hoping that my dear collaborator tidied this up in the end, because as of writing several days after the final draft was sent to the editors, I still haven't seen MA's side of the manuscript.

And last I read in Michael 3 there seemed to be something going on with Sabine and Akio.

But Akio is gay. Right?

Confused, and hopeful, I posted this on fb:

QUESTION:

Did anyone else read Michael #3 and think that there was something heating up between Sabine and Akio?

Or was it just me (projecting)?

Need to know. MA giving me shit... and potentially missing a very real thread that needs to be tied up.

The response was huge.

To begin with I was told that I was just projecting.

However, as the thread gained momentum there was an overwhelming majority of folks who also had the impression that there was something going on: at least on Sabine's side. And if it was all one sided, well Akio still needed some romantic action of whatever persuasion the Author chose to give him.

So while I am comforted that it "wasn't just me", I'm also mildly concerned that MA has sent this to the editing team without addressing this thread.

Because, like, it's *romance*.

And while he's all down with the killy-killy, he keeps telling me he's not into doing the kissy-kissy writing thing.

(He'll be blushing as he reads this. And when we read it out on the audio recording, you'll probably wanna go check the video!)

<Michael Edit: Yeah, I'm not into the kissy-kissy at all. I'll do fade to black scenes where the next time you see them, they will be talking after all the action.>

Anyway – I'm sure y'all'll let me know in the amazon reviews or indeed on my fb page what the verdict was.

I'm not holding my breath for any romantic conclusion though.

The other cool thing about actually going back and reading the other half of the story is that you realize all the shit your collaborator pulled.

Like modelling the evil scientists on the exact same mannerisms that he's teased you about. And when I mentioned it, everyone else clocked that too!

Sigh.

The crap I put up with…

Ellie and Giles

So one of the things I realized over the last few weeks is that not everyone has the same taste in characters I do.

I like 'em (like my men): broken yet evolving.

Like Molly.

Or Giles.

So when the Giles series didn't take off like gangbusters I was kinda surprised.

But then MA and I figured a few things out:

1. We didn't do the rapid release. Book 1, 2, then 3 all within the space of a month.
2. Not everyone understood the Giles character.
3. Those that kinda got him thought: yeah he's interesting… But he's also kind of a jerk. In talking to a number of folks since it seems that

his charm in the early Molly books wasn't
enough to counteract his douchiness.

Now, for those who have read **Confessions of a Space Archeologist: Rogue Operator**, and some of the Molly books where he appears (book 5 onwards) you start to see more of him. It was our hope in Michael 4 and the Epilogue that you'd get to see some of his backstory.

i.e. What prompts an archeologist to nomad across the galaxies, looking to get his ya-yas out Indiana Jones style. What is he searching for… literally, and emotionally? Why is he missing the mark? What isn't he getting?

What you're seeing in this book is a little of what makes him want to go off and touch other civilizations.

And as you probably figured out, he has a huge heart.

A heart that feels deeply.

But because of this sensitivity he has to protect it any way he can.

And the way he choses? Well, with an over inflated ego and addiction to adventure, of course :)

For those who are already waiting for Giles 2 you'll see him evolve out of this to the point where he starts making the connections within his own psyche, and "getting it". And of course there is the same amount of killy-killy badassery and carnage that goes along side him unravelling a mystery with snark and humour. All typical TKG stuff you've come to expect.

If you'd like to read more about Giles, go check out his series, book 1:

Confessions of a Space Archeologist: Rogue Operator

.   .   .

By the time you're through that, book 2 will be hitting the 'Zon, under the title: **Rogue Instigator**.

Ellie, Hopes 'N Dreams

As the Michael and Bethany Anne series draw to a close, we're being asked: what next?

Ellie Translation: **where can I get my next fix?**

And it's a good question.

So let me address this as far as what I'm privy to…

Ellie, MA and their Future: Ranger #2

I've just, as I've been writing this, realized why MA calls Tabitha "Ranger Two".

All this time I was thinking that this was some sort of half-baked sequel he wanted me to work on.

And then (like five seconds ago as I typed the subhead here) it dawned on me that in the same way that they each have a number… Like Barnabas is #1 and Sean/Johnny is #7… Tabitha must be #2.

Face palm. Doh.

I'm so fucking slow sometimes. #FML.

Hahahahahaha.

<Michael Edit: Seriously? I've only explained this at least a couple of times, and *READ YOU* the scene where Meredith Nicole Grimes pulls out Tabitha's Ranger 2 symbol. Apparently, I'm not listened to very well.>

Anyway… all this to say, for those who have been asking about when MA and I will be writing together again, the next series we have planned in a Ranger #2 series.

(We're going to have to talk about how to name it… coz this Ranger shitty-sequel-two-thing clearly isn't working in my brain. Omg do I feel like a Muppet!)

I'm sure, now I've verbalized this internal anxiety, we'll be able to talk about it and come up with something awesome.

<Michael Edit: Like maybe "Ranger *002?*">

Until then, this is the working title.

It's basically going to see Tabitha, and her wild child of a niece, Nikki, tell their stories, each separated by about 150 years but thematically entwined. It's gonna be a challenge, I'm sure.

<Michael Edit: Technically, It's Jean and John Grimes' granddaughter, but everyone in "that" group, including Tabitha, treat each others kids as their niece and nephews.>

It's all first person and very killy-killy with lots of swearing and action. Action of the fighting variety. And probably the other variety too… At least in off-screen suggestions, coz well, MA says that Nikki is very… erm… sexual? I think that was his word.

Anyway….

I get to write the wild child side. (Yup, the sweary, slutty, badass, futuristic version of Tabby-cat).

Needlesstosay I'm going to have to research this area. I may even have to play a game "what would wild child, off-the-rails Nikki do"?

And being in Austin… well, that's the ultimate playground.

Maybe Austin will become known as my Nikki Ranger days??

Who knows.

Until then, watch this space, stay awesome, and Ad Aeternitatem.

Ellie x

Receive updates from Oz by registering your holo/email address here:
ellleighclarke.com

The Ascension Myth
*** With Michael Anderle ***

Awakened (01)

Activated (02)

Called (03)

Sanctioned (04)

Rebirth (05)

Retribution (06)

Cloaked (07)

Bourne (08)

Committed (09)

Subversion (10)

Invasion (11)

Ascension (12)

Confessions of a Space Anthropologist
*** With Michael Anderle ***

Giles Kurns: Rogue Operator (1)

Giles Kurns: Rogue Instigator (2)

The Second Dark Ages

www.ingramcontent.com/pod-product-compliance
Lightning Source LLC
Chambersburg PA
CBHW070627100726
47907CB00007B/1889